HEAVEN
AND
EARTH

by

GUIDO CASALE

Grosvenor House
Publishing Limited

This book is published by
Grosvenor House Publishing Ltd
28-30 High Street, Guildford, Surrey, GU1 3EL.
www.grosvenorhousepublishing.co.uk

A CIP record for this book
is available from the British Library

ISBN 978-1-78148-746-4

This book is dedicated to
Valerie with much love

Peig Sayers, a traditional storyteller who lived on the Great Blasket Island off the coast of Kerry [and whom I knew as an old lady when I was a child] was once asked where heaven was. In reply, she said it was just a few inches above the tallest man in the island. Heaven and earth, like life and death, were one in the traditional way of thinking. Whether or not Peig realised it, her belief about heaven's closeness to earth is very similar to the thinking of the great medieval mystic known as Meister Eckhart. When he was asked where the soul of a person goes after death, Eckhart said, "No place. Where else would the soul be going? Where else is the eternal world? It can be nowhere other than here."

[From *'Now Is The Time : Spiritual
Reflections'*
by Stanislaus Kennedy]

"Doctor,
If only you could see
How heaven pulls earth into its arms
And how infinitely the heart expands
to claim this world, blue vapor without end."

[From *'Monet Refuses The Operation'*
by Lisel Mueller]

TEN YEARS EARLIER

 Donna lay in bed listening to the strange creaky silence of the house, her body clammy and reluctant to concede to sleep. What had happened to the foxes these last few nights? she wondered. Her thoughts turned towards Tony and became instantly tinged with disappointment. She had hoped he might come and watch her compete in the school sports next week. "Sorry, mate," he had apologised earlier that day, his eyes fixed dolefully on the flood tide of the river. "I'll be at the factory making butterflies. Another time, eh?"

It had been their elusive neighbour, Tony, who had told her about the foxes, how they came skulking out of their dens on the railway embankments and took nocturnal possession of the residential gardens, how savagely they fought each other for territorial rights. He had put a name and a reason to the supernatural yowls of rage that broke her terrified out of slumber.

Suddenly the door clicked open and Donna rolled over just in time to catch the spectral figure of her sister duck beneath the frame of the bunks. It juddered and settled in the darkness. "Sarah?" she said but only a solitary aeroplane droned distantly in response. "Sarah? You're not allowed to be here." No reply. "Unless you're going to tell me about daddy?" she threatened. The silence resumed, hard and opaque. "I'm going to call mummy now and she'll make you go back to your own room."

"Please don't do that," came the reply from below. "I was having a bad dream." Donna felt her heart swell with pity. "What causes dreams, Sarah?" she asked at length. "Where do they come from?"

"Can I get into your bed?" replied Sarah and the frame creaked as the uninvited guest scrambled up the pine ladder. The mattress sagged beneath the implosion of unexpected weight. "You're not allowed!" objected Donna. "Shush, keep your voice down," whispered Sarah. "You'll wake mummy. Move over a bit. That's better. God, you're sticky." A smell of cold cream and peppermint pervaded Donna's nostrils.

"Why doesn't mummy put any photos of daddy on the mantelpiece?" demanded Donna. "She prefers to keep them hidden away," came the muted reply. "Didn't mummy love him, Sarah?" Silence. "Sarah?" A snort of impatience then, "Course she loved him, div. She's scared, I reckon." Donna felt puzzled. "Scared of what?" she asked. "I don't know. The past I suppose. She thinks he cheated on her with other women – but he didn't. I spent more time with daddy than she did. And even if he did, it was mummy's own fault. She never stopped nagging him about getting a proper job."

Donna heard Sarah's voice falter with emotion but she twisted a strand of hair round her index finger and pressed on regardless. "I'd love to see a photo of our daddy," she said. "Were there any of him and me?" Silence. "Sarah, were you there when daddy died?" Silence. "What happened? Sarah?" "You know very well," muttered Sarah reluctantly. "Mummy told you." "But that was a long time ago," whined Donna. "I can't really remember. Was I asleep in my pram? Sarah? Tell me."

Sarah turned over and Donna could feel her sister's breathing right next to her ear. "I've got a picture of daddy holding you at your christening party," whispered Sarah. "I'll show you tomorrow. He'd won some money on a horse race," reminisced Sarah. "Who?" interrupted Donna carelessly and got an elbow in her ribs as reward. "*I'm just popping out to the shops*, he said," continued Sarah. "I wanted to go with him. He wouldn't let me at first. But I insisted. Kicked up a fuss, I suppose. *For God's sake take her, Don*, called mummy, *before she wakes up the baby*. He'd already left and I had to run after him through the front door. The shops were on a really busy road. The south circular it's called. And I wasn't allowed there on my own. *I'll buy you some sweets*, he told me. *Go back in now*. But I wanted my own way. *Let me come with you and choose*, I kept pestering. By that time we had reached the corner and he had to bend down to speak to me above the noise of the traffic thundering past. *Just tell me the name of the sweeties you want and I'll buy them*, he said. I told him the names of a couple of things. *Okay, straight home*, he grinned and pointed. I turned round and pretended to go but then I remembered something else I wanted and walked back after him. Daddy was already marching off towards the zebra crossing."

Donna envisaged it like a film running in her head, a film she had seen before but whose horrible details she had pushed to the remotest corner of memory. "*Daddy!* I shouted," Sarah continued with increasing emotion. "*Can you get me a packet of Lovehearts too?* He seemed to half hear and hesitate, looking back towards me, grinning, and sort of waving with a thumb turned up......and then he walked on to the crossing, still looking in my direction, and there was this.....this sudden long screech like an animal in pain.....I think daddy must have looked round to see what it was...... and as he did he just seemed to fold up and disappear into the ground. And where he'd been was this enormous truck."

The sobs and groans of wrenching anguish began quietly at first then slowly accumulated to a crescendo. Donna had heard them before but never like this. Now she could feel them against her body. They belonged to her too. "It was my fault," Sarah whimpered. "No it wasn't," Donna objected. "Daddy wasn't looking properly. He should have been." But this offer of respite would not satisfy Sarah. "That's what Dr Williamson keeps telling me," she replied. "But I know it was my fault. I killed our daddy and he died in horrible pain."

Wave upon wave of grief reared up again and crashed down in the darkness. All Donna could do was cling on to the black rock of her sister's body and search her memory for words of consolation. "I love you, Sarah," she said. "The doctors would have given daddy drugs to stop the pain and make him dream lovely things, they would."

Much later in the very pit of night when Donna was stirred by a hideously prolonged noise her first thought was that it belonged to a dream – the shrieking, panic-stricken brakes of the recycling truck - then it repeated locally right outside the window and she realised instantly the cause. "Sarah? Listen. It's the foxes," she whispered. But her sister's breathing did not falter. Donna sensed how completely Sarah had let go of the world and all the inexplicable tortures contained therein and sunk too far down to be reached by even the most tender of voices. She listened to the dreadful cacophony totally unafraid. After a couple of minutes it ceased as abruptly as it had begun and the vast abyss of sleep swallowed her up too.

TIME AND ETERNITY

 Barbara Martelli felt suddenly crumpled as she emerged from the taxi onto a wet London pavement close to the Inns of Court. No doubt vitality would return once she took the rostrum. Initially Martelli's part-time job as an emeritus professor of Social Psychology had felt like a sinecure, a way of gently back-peddling into retirement rather than suddenly dismounting from the academic bicycle only to discover her septuagenarian body had forgotten the habit of standing on its own two feet. In addition the post had allowed her time to pursue certain research activities that, if the Academy had known about them officially, might well have occasioned ripples of disapproval. But now, having attained great grandmotherly status, Professor Martelli no longer cared whose feathers she ruffled. She had handed in her notice and a date of departure amicably agreed.

The author of several major publications Martelli's latest one, *Heaven And Earth*, would constitute a literary swansong. It was not addressed to an elite inner sanctum of intellectuals, a fact that had pleased her publisher who hoped the book might enflame the popular reading imagination in the same way Lyall Watson's *Supernature* once had. Profits did not concern Martelli. She was using the book to cast out a global net like a fisherman to entice whatever exotic creatures dwelled in the mysterious ocean depths to find a safe haven on board her ship. Consequently she had agreed to a promotional series of public lectures and interviews spread over a period of three months. If sales took off a further lecture tour of North America would go ahead.

So here she stood near the portals of The London School of Economics' new academic building, an inconspicuous grey-haired figure wearing a blue raincoat, looking slightly lost until someone approached and brashly asked her if she would like to become a millionaire. Almost simultaneously another man butted in, introducing himself as the pro vice chancellor and escorted her safely away. In the foyer of the vast Sheik Zayed Lecture Theatre a dedicated bookstall had been specially erected, piled high with all the guest speaker's titles. A buzz of anticipation filled the air and a long queue was filing through the entrance. As Martelli passed by it she received several knowing smiles. "How are you, Barbara?" someone asked solicitously and reminded her of his name. "Martin Williamson. You mentored me once. It must be twenty- five years since we last met!" She chatted with him briefly then the dean ushered her into a private hospitality room where sherry awaited.

Sarah Atkinson, fifty years Martelli's junior, had already secured a front of house seat and a copy of *Heaven And Earth*. She too had been subjected to the 'would you like to become a millionaire?' question on the arrival precinct. An American wearing an expensive executive suit had offered her free entry to a seminar run by one Luke Karamba called 'How to become very rich in seven easy steps'. All he wanted in exchange was Sarah's name and email address. She had scanned the leaflet he handed her and asked, "How do I know you are not just a dangerous pervert?" The man's synthetic smile broadened. "Luke is a Seventh-day Adventist," he replied. "He saves souls as well as makes them rich. And if you haven't earned £25,000 profit in the first three months of your business operation, Miss, in return for an audited account of the deficit he will personally reimburse you the balance. That's how confident Luke is he can make you wealthy. Your name and email address please?" Sarah crumpled the flyer in her hand. "Just as I thought," she had laughed as she walked away. "You are a dangerous pervert."

As the audience trundled in slowly Sarah perused the opening pages of Martelli's book. It was organised in sections as follows: Time and Eternity, Innocence and Experience, Dreams and Reality, Sanity and Madness, Truth and Falsehood, Feeling and Thought, Freedom and Captivity, Science and Religion, Life and Death, Darkness and Light, Heaven and Earth. "A chimpanzee has 99% of the same genes humans have," began the introduction, "but unlike us a chimp has no linguistic facility and therefore no thought processes, no imagination and no creativity. The ape does have one thing we do not possess, however, and that is an unambiguous sense of its species being. A chimp is a chimp. It can be no other. It may be frightened or frustrated at times but not in the way we are, psychologically and spiritually. It does not conjecture, 'Why am I here? What is my life's purpose?' It does not fret about its mortality, nor anguish about the black hole of oblivion waiting to swallow up its achievements and relationships. A chimp has no sense of time passing. When Wittgenstein wrote, 'If we take eternity to mean not infinite temporal duration but timelessness, then eternal life belongs to those who live in the present,' I think he probably had a chimp in mind.

"I am not quite a chimpanzee although I sometimes wish I were, given the direction in which scientific civilisation seems to be frantically accelerating. A chimp can unpeel a banana, imitate basic gestures it witnesses and secure a territorial space but these are not consciously creative acts, rather instinctive ones. A chimp cannot write poetry, harness electromagnetism or expound theories like evolution and the big bang; neither however can a chimpanzee bomb Japanese cities into nuclear extinction, create a hole in the ozone layer, exterminate six million Jews in labour camps or participate in the kind of miraculous synchronicity that saved my parents from exactly that fate. You see my father was an Italian Jew, my mother an Austrian Jewess. They were both opera singers who met and fell in love while working at a Viennese theatre in the years when Nazism was rapidly gaining popular support. During a production of *The Magic Flute* that did not require my mother's participation Papageno took my father aside backstage. 'I tell you this because I like you,' he confided. 'They are watching you closely. In a week's time it may be too late.' When father arrived home he found mother already asleep in bed so it was not until the following morning he tried to tell her about the bizarre warning. 'Wait,' she arrested him. 'I must tell you first about a terrible dream I had in the night. There were hideous corpses piled up all around me. Suddenly one of them stood up and spoke to me. His clothes were arrayed in the plumage of birds. *I tell you this because I like you*, he said grimly. *They are watching you closely. In a week's time it may be too late.*' That was Friday. On Monday my parents began the long trek to England where I was to be born eighteen months later - "

Suddenly the microphone spluttered into life and a man began haranguing the now three-quarters full auditorium in a way that had nothing to do with the guest lecturer. So far as Sarah could tell amidst the outbreak of heckles, the speaker was an academic victim of an enforced redundancy programme petitioning his erstwhile colleagues for concerted resistance. Martin Williamson could hardly believe his eyes. He recognised the interloper as Edgar Laidlaw, one of his most idiosyncratic clients, and Williamson was wondering whether to intervene when a couple of security guards wrestled the protester out of the theatre to accompanying ironic applause.

Sarah resumed her reading: "Growing up with a family story like that for company it should not surprise you to know that I became precociously interested in the bizarre nature of human consciousness. Patricia, my best friend at High School, could make her pencil stand up and waggle across the desk simply by concentrating hard and giving it an order. She had a small repertoire of such mind over matter tricks that I alone was privileged to witness. But when she was fourteen the inanimate objects suddenly ceased obeying Patricia's mental commands. My later reading informed me that such 'paranormal' activity was quite common in the vicinity of prepubescent girls. Conventional science's best guess explanation for the phenomenon was that pent-up sexual energy caused it to happen, although how exactly it could not elaborate. Science, as I came to realise by the age of 21, has no final explanations for many phenomena. Like Jack Haldane, the geneticist I was privileged to get to know at UCL where I took my doctorate, I realised 'the universe is not only queerer than we suppose, but queerer than we *can* suppose.' The other thing I realised is that the overarching phenomenon we are generally pleased to call 'reality' is a social construction created by, and mainly for the benefit of, men.

"My doctorate research was just a continuation of my childhood curiosity about the nature of consciousness. Is consciousness different from sentience and, if so, how exactly? Is consciousness a purely physical property of the brain that emanates thoughts in the same way an electric fire emanates heat? Why has self-consciousness evolved in humans and what are its creative challenges? My search for answers took me first to Biology and Physics then to Psychology and Anthropology and finally to Religion, Mysticism and the Occult.

I became a convert to what the astrophysicist, Edgar Mitchell, later came to call Noetic Science. I realised we humans tap into only a very small fraction of the innate potential of our consciousness and indeed we are afraid to do so. If that fear could be dissipated humanity would be launched into realms of problem solving and invention that are currently regarded as impossible by scientific orthodoxy. Our capacity for self-actualisation, both collectively and individually, would become virtually unbounded. The wickedness and selfishness that blights our world might be ended."

After the lecture Sarah headed for the cafeteria and purchased a drink. The squat little space containing ten tables was packed but she managed to squeeze into a spare chair. "Did you enjoy her talk?" smiled the man sitting opposite, folding up a newspaper. Sarah responded with a quizzical expression. The man pointed at her book. "I finished it yesterday," he explained. "I came here prepared for an argument but Martelli covered all her most contentious bases pretty well."

He was quite handsome, Sarah noticed, and impeccably dressed with black hair, sympathetic brown eyes and delicate oriental features. "I was a bit disappointed there is no section in the book called 'Male and Female'," she remarked. "I think you'll find that is the connecting theme unifying the whole discourse," he opined. "At least it was for me, anyway." The man looked away now quite shyly and Sarah felt a sudden sense of loneliness emanating from him. For half an hour they chatted about the psychology of consciousness, creation myths, synchronicities, the relativity of space-time and the physiology of the brain. "Scientific studies of the brain are all inconclusive," opined Sarah.

"I tend to agree," nodded the man who had introduced himself as Johnnie Woo, a native of Hong Kong now domiciled in London. "And there is no valid reason to assume that organic life preceded consciousness; or that consciousness ends with physical death - as counterintuitive as that sounds. As Jung intimated, consciousness might well turn out to be another force of nature. Forgive my curiosity, who was it that died very recently? Your father?"

"My mother actually," confessed Sarah. "Dad died much longer ago when I was six. You're either telepathic or a good guesser." Johnnie shrugged modestly that he sometimes experienced such intuitions. "Bet you can't intuit what I'm going to ask you next though?" Sarah grinned. "May I borrow your Guardian? I want to check they've published my advert." She found the insertion, handed the newspaper back and stood up to leave. "I've enjoyed your company," she said. "You are very easy to talk to – " And was about to add, "for a man" but bit her tongue. "Maybe we could meet up again for a drink sometime?" she suggested.

"I'd like that very much," replied Johnnie. Sarah scribbled her number on a till receipt for him and departed before Johnnie had a chance to reciprocate.

 Immediately after the lecture Barbara Martelli took a taxi home. She lived in Islington just south of Upper Street, alone – except when one or more of her grandchildren came to stay. It was a large house for a widow, even one whose collection of books and manuscripts ran into tens of thousands. She placed her supper in the oven and browsed through the newspaper while it cooked. Suddenly she saw it. **DON ATKINSON**. The name in dark upper case followed by *Australian writer, actor and comedian. Died 1989. Married to Margaret. Information kindly requested from anyone who knew him by his elder daughter, Sarah.* A box number was appended.

Martelli had a photo somewhere of Penny and Don together and when she finally rifled it out of a drawer tears began to form in her eyes. How young and innocent they look! And dead within a few days of each other! After supper she went to her study. Her cataloguing system was impeccable. Martelli threw nothing away. She simply moved stuff around, re-prioritised it in cabinets and boxes. This is what had happened to Don's collection. She had not thought about it, nor read any of it for years. As she opened the cabinet drawer her heart fluttered with trepidation. It felt like unearthing a tomb and resurrecting the dead after almost two decades of sleep. The quantity of paper material bulked larger than she remembered. And a couple of video cassettes. What should she do? Here was a legacy to which Don's children were indisputably entitled but once she had dispatched it an avalanche of potentially distracting questions would almost certainly rebound on her head and the privacy Martelli guarded so carefully compromised. She chewed the dilemma over methodically with her meal.

Two other people with special interest had noticed Sarah's advert. One of them named Reginald Cookson sat in an airport departure lounge awaiting his flight to Sidney to be called. "I must remember to contact her when I get back to the UK," he told himself. The second was Martin Williamson who had already received two letters from Miss Atkinson and neglected to answer them, partly because their substance awoke unhappy memories for him but also because Sarah had been for him the antithesis of her mother, Margaret, - in short a stroppy, self-centred adolescent.

That night as he read *Heaven And Earth* Williamson could not prevent the image of Margaret Atkinson from infecting his concentration. The news of her passing had sorely troubled his heart like no other loss he had known. He was half way through a chapter entitled *Time And Eternity* that examined the evidence, such as it existed, for reincarnation and the continuation of life after physical demise. In purchasing Martelli's book had he been desperately grasping at some system of consolation to pit against his perennial atheism? he wondered. Nowadays Williamson found himself ruminating frequently about death and he was not sure why. Maybe it was just a temporary life change issue? His business partners had been trying to foist a premature retirement deal on him, generous in financial terms if not in existential ones. So perhaps it was the thought of a professional void beckoning that perturbed him? He already had a domestic one to endure, unmarried and childless as he was. Or perhaps something else irked him, something opaque and malevolent in his nature that he could not consciously face up to? He put the book down and selected another more likely to lift his mood, he felt, an autobiographical account of her early life in Lancashire by Jeanette Winterson called *Why Be Happy When You Could Be Normal.*

The next morning being a Friday Williamson's appointments' secretary, Silvia, ran through his schedule of the following week's meetings. Every name mentioned struck a distinctive chord in the memory. It was strange being a psychotherapist, the way with your clients you gradually moved from anonymity to familiarity and finally towards intimacy, the space between encounters, the strategies you employed for dismantling defensive barriers. No two clients were the same. In some cases nothing close to an intimate connection occurred, in other cases there were memorably productive connections, and just once there had occurred an epiphany – a series of encounters so comprehensibly fruitful that they had transformed for better or worse the analyst's own life.

He tried to repress the urge to grimace as Silvia mentioned Edgar Laidlaw's name. "It's his final consultation of twelve," she added. "A discharge report will have to be subsequently sent to his ex-employer." That brought back a smile of relief to Williamson's face. Six months and it had been tough going. The first occasion Laidlaw consulted Williamson he had arrived ten minutes after the appointment time and been politely informed of his transgression.

He remembered this now as he gazed at the city landscape from his tenth floor south bank window. "There's no such thing as time, you know," Laidlaw had smirked. "Time is an invention of the human mind, an attempt to impose order where none exists. What clock-watchers like you call time is actually chronology. It is an artificial reckoning system. You may just as well measure out your life with coffee spoons as hours and minutes. Of course I'll grant you there is ageing and dying but that happens outside of time not because of it. What time do you make it?"

'Four thirteen," replied Williamson with a glance at his watch.

"That is not the correct answer," smiled Laidlaw. "The correct answer is now. It is always now, Mr Williamson. Never ten past now or quarter to now. Just now. Do you prefer mister of doctor?"

"I don't mind," answered the analyst.

"I shall call you mister then," said the client. "I find doctor a bit over-stated. It's not as if you can perform open-heart surgery or diagnose sciatica, is it? I am sure you must have heard the phrase 'the power of now'? To exist in the now moment is to be fully human. To exist at four thirteen or at whatever the digits of your watch indicate is to be merely a mechanically directed contrivance. The more we allow our timepieces to dictate the longevity and quality of our actions the more we develop the characteristics of those timepieces."

Williamson looked the client closely in the eyes. "Would you please tell me for what purpose you made this appointment?" he said.

"Of course," replied Laidlaw. "I never thought you were going to ask! I'd like six months worth of one hour consultations at fortnightly inter-vals. How much will they cost?" Williamson explained that he charged two hundred pounds per consultation. "Any discounts for block booking?" asked the client. The analyst shook his head. "I suspected not. I'll take it. Beggars can't be choosers. And it'll help me keep fit."

"I don't follow."

"In order to meet your rather exorbitant costs I shall need to give up a few luxuries such as Burgundy wine and using London transport. But no matter, it shall be worth it," said Laidlaw. When Williamson reassured him there were many cheaper analysts around the client quipped, "I sincerely hope so for the sake of the great unwashed! However your practice was specified by the distinguished panjandrum to whom I am indebted for my liberty and his decision cannot be gainsaid. Oh look, I notice from your watch I've spent fifty pounds already! My last bottle of Chateauneuf du Pape is going to taste extra good tonight. Do you imbibe, Mr Williamson? I sort of felt that being a shrink was such a stressful job you would definitely need to?"

It transpired Laidlaw's attendance at psychotherapy had been forced on him as the consequence of an informal judicial arrangement. Enraged by the university's redundancy scheme the senior lecturer in art history had physically jostled his boss. The police were called but the vice chancellor, being of a Christian persuasion, eventually offered to drop the charges if Laidlaw agreed to undergo anger management counselling. For the perpetrator such generosity was a no-brainer. He passed a letter to the analyst that was quickly read. "Do you accept the vice-chancellor's description of you here as an angry and compulsive person?" asked Williamson.

"I certainly do," beamed Laidlaw. "I proudly accept it. Whosoever is not angry is purblind to the barbarity of the epoch. In this post modern, neo-liberal asylum we inhabit the real crime is insouciance and complicity, don't you think, not the righteously angry urge to denounce it?"

"I suppose the vice chancellor's point is about the pugilistic manner in which you did so?" observed Williamson.

Laidlaw did not appear to hear the question. It was as if the utterance of the words 'post modern' and 'neo-liberal' had simultaneously reopened a deep suppurating wound in his sensibility and he began rambling on about dodgy financial derivatives, the fraudulent selling of PPIs, the fixing of the libor rate and other transgressions committed by the banks and financial services industry. From there it was an easy rhetorical journey to the many multinational organisations which he referred to collectively as 'the corrupt unaccountable state within the global state,' to the obscene self-serving apathy of the political elite, the criminal dismantling of the welfare system and the deliberate smokescreen of a phoney war on terrorism to distract the attention of the masses. "The real terror is within us, within our hearts and minds," Laidlaw ranted. "We are ugly, greedy, brutish beings and we choose not to see it. One tiny sneaky peep into the mirror of our inner nature and the glass would instantly crack with shame!"

"But you look into it and what you see makes you violently angry," proposed Williamson. "Is that good for your long term health?"

"You remind me of my wife, Christabelle," chuckled the client. "She was prettier than you and less hirsute, of course. But she spoke in a similarly patronising way. After two years of marriage she told me I was a misfit, misogynist and malingerer, and then left me. She liked words that began with M. It was a devastating experience."

"Mallingerer? Why did she call you that?" asked Williamson.

"An excellent question!" exclaimed Laidlaw. "I'm beginning to enjoy this! It enervated me. It totally depleted me of energy. It rendered me comatose and legless for long periods."

"It?" queried Williamson raising an eyebrow. "What is *it*?"

The client flung his left arm towards the window. "The meretricious sprawl out there, the rat race thing!" he ejaculated. "Well not just that alone, the fact I was supposed to be a participant in its meaningless dance of death. I became physically ill."

"But you eventually recovered, I assume?" said Williamson.

"Correct. I found the key to the wormhole that led from the brutish world of time and the ephemeral to the permanent world of art and the eternal. Am I boring you, Mr Williamson? That wasn't a yawn you were just trying to stifle?" The analyst shook his head and, once reassured, Laidlaw continued his story. "I cannot say how exactly it happened. All I know is that one day I was standing in this purgatorial culture of Mammon and the next a trap door seemed to pop open in my consciousness and I plunged as it were downwards into a timeless wonderland. I now know many others have been on the same journey. We may refer to them as visionaries and artists to distinguish them from the vivisectionists and money-crunchers such as you whose grinding application to the machinery of the material world keep the myth of civilisation alive. I am not an artist myself, it goes without saying. I never had sufficient skill. But I know a genuine artist when I see their work. So to return to that eternal wonderland, to escape the ravages of time, all I need to do is, for example, look at a Monet or Van Gogh painting or listen to a Bach double violin concerto or The Verdi Requiem. Utterly heavenly experiences! Mr Williamson, you look less than convinced? Let me assure you Vincent's paintings of sunflowers and of even his chair are more real than the originals, so transfigured have they become in the heat of the artist's attentiveness! You may appreciate how my job as an art historian became my salvation, therefore, and how to be deprived of it in six months will be, at the very least, inconvenient. Not just to me personally, I must emphasise, but to all those young people for whom I could have been a conduit on their own personal journeys to eternity."

At the conclusion of that first consultation Williamson had created a new client file and written in it, *Initial impression: intense, judgemental, articulate, over-confident, bitter and highly opinionated. Perhaps the lady doth protest too much? Suspect an impractical and naïve side to his nature. Check this out.*

A sharp knock on the door broke the therapist out of his reverie. It was Silvia wearing a perplexed expression. "I've got a Miss Sarah Atkinson on the phone," she said, "and she is quite adamant that she needs to speak to you. Shall I put her through?"

Williamson considered briefly. "Tell her I'm busy," he said. "Tell her I'll ring her back later."

INNOCENCE
AND EXPERIENCE

 Sarah was vexed with disappointment at not having received a single reply to her advert when, ten days later on a crowded commuter train home from Waterloo, a man boarding at Clapham Junction arrested her attention. He huddled in the standing area close to the doors. She had noticed him before recently and the impression of who he might be had gradually begun to coalesce in her memory. After a couple more stations seats became vacated and the man took one directly opposite to her. "Excuse me, I may be making a mistake," she addressed him, "but are you by any chance called Richard?" She hesitated on the surname. "I can't quite remember your second name, sorry."

The man's jowly middle-aged face relaxed into a gratified smile. He liked attractive young women. "Richard Weller," he replied, leaning forwards. "And who might you be?"

"Sarah Atkinson," she announced. "You were a friend of my dad, Don." Weller looked blank. "I'm sure you played tennis with him?"

Weller furrowed his brow. "I played tennis with a lot of people, pretty badly, too," he remarked with a comedic wince. "When exactly was this?"

Sarah did a quick calculation. "In the eighties. We went round to your house once and I think you came to my sister Donna's christening party. You and your wife, Penny, is it? And I think you had three kids?"

"It's a long time ago," sighed Weller. "Since then I've lived mainly in the far east and Canada. The old grey matter is no longer what it used to be, I'm afraid, Sarah." Sarah allowed the conversation to lapse into silence and, as the train pulled into Richmond, Weller stood up to disembark. "Well, this is my stop," he smiled. "Do give my regards to your dad."

For a brief moment Sarah considered following him off the train and challenging the authenticity of his amnesia. But it seemed genuine enough. There had been no coldness or hostility – just something else more brittle and factitious. By the time Sarah alighted at the next station, St Margaret's, she had identified it. "Trauma," she thought recalling a quotation that she had heard somewhere, perhaps in the Martelli lecture. "Trauma creates its own mask, its own impervious texture of protective insulation."

When she arrived home Sarah found her sister loafing in the garden with a drawing pad and friend. "What are you doing?" she demanded accusingly.

"Drawing Mike's portrait," answered Donna without diluting the concentration of her gaze. "You remember Mike, don't you? He's studying Anthropology at Sussex University now. I was just telling him about those boomerang word code games you taught me to play."

"Did she tell you what an innocently trusting member of the tribe she is, too," replied Sarah sarcastically for Mike's benefit. "How she once befriended a dangerous ex-con who'd nicked ten million quid's worth of gold bullion? You're not secretly a felon yourself, by any chance?" Mike offered an embarrassed grin and shook his head in confusion. "Good," snapped Sarah. "Until I discover otherwise I'll assume your intentions towards Donna are just lasciviously dishonourable then. What a life it is being a college student!" she scolded her sister. "I especially left The Guardian for you and a list of jobs."

"All done," retorted Donna. "You're not my mother, Sarah, and I'm still on Easter holiday. By the way, someone called Johnnie rang for you. Didn't catch his surname. And Jocelyn as well, just back from abroad. She's received letters from several new applicants wanting to join The Unreasonable Club and needs your help contacting them."

Sarah betrayed a gratified smile then muttered something pompous about the importance of books and serious reading as she retreated back to the house. There's nothing wrong with not liking reading, Donna thought. Not everyone can be an egghead and a part-time Sociology tutor. In fact Donna had spent over an hour after finishing the housework browsing first through the newspaper then her final assignment notes on Van Gogh before the sheer monsoon of hieroglyphics overwhelmed her brain and she felt she was about to drown in verbiage.

"What's The Unreasonable Club?" asked the portrait sitter. "So far as I can tell," replied Donna, "it's where angry women go to let off steam." Mike eyed her cautiously and said, "But you're not a member, I take it?" The nervous tick that accompanied this question launched Donna into a fit of giggles. "Call me old fashioned," she recovered herself, "but I can't think of anything to be angry about."

Donna felt compelled to apologise to Mike for her sister's abrasive manner and to offer him a potted history of Sarah's childhood waywardness. A counsellor friend of their mother's called Dr Williamson had been enlisted at critical times to try to keep Sarah on the rails, she explained, but Sarah had never taken to him. "When Sarah was seventeen and about to ditch advanced level study she was introduced to Jocelyn by her college tutor and bingo, something just clicked between them," continued Donna. "Joc worked for an organisation called MIND. She was seriously into gender politics, and since then they've become big mates. Hold your head still, Mike. That's it. But recently Sarah's developed this mission thing about dad. You see mum never spoke about dad much because it upset her. But now Sarah feels free to poke her nose into all the hidden family corners of the past. It's like she believes there's some mystery needs unravelling."

After Mike had gone home, Donna remembered something else she had to tell Sarah. "A huge parcel arrived by special courier. I left it in the box room," she said going to recover it. "Who is it from? Have you been buying on eBay again?"

"No," muttered Sarah ripping into the packaging and suddenly revealing a collection of old wire bound notebooks. They emanated a fusty smell and seemed to suffuse her curious fingertips with the tactile energy of history. No covering letter had been attached. Tentatively she picked the first book up and studied the pages, full of dense neat handwriting. "Bloody hell!" she gasped in astonishment.

"Sarah? What is it?" said Donna anxiously and peered over her sister's shoulder. Inside the cover the notebook's owner had identified himself. *Don Atkinson*, she read. *England 1979.*

 On Sunday morning Martin Williamson awoke from a lurid nightmare haunted by both Margaret and Don Atkinson. In the dream Williamson had drowned after falling off a bridge and been taken to meet them by Edgar Laidlaw in what seemed to be an antechamber of paradise. For a few waking seconds Williamson recognised with absolute lucidity the true nature of the person he was, a revelation so traumatic that it had to be instantaneously eclipsed from his conscious mind.

Five miles away Sarah Atkinson had been dreaming too but far more pleasantly. She had fallen asleep under the spell of a tale unearthed in one of Don's notebooks. Stories, jokes, poetry, dramatic dialogue plus random ideas and musings as well as the routine autobiographical stuff of diaries, all neatly handwritten, filled over 1400 pages of twelve spiral bound journals. They represented the workshop of a writer whose career had also involved acting and stand-up comedy. She had been browsing for ages when a single word gripped her attention. *Boomerang*. Don used to tell her funny bedtime stories about the secret life of a boy with that peculiar nickname who communicated to his friends in coded language. Don had even explained to little Sarah the rudiments of written ciphers and indeed "boomerang" had become their private code word, meaning "danger ahead!" or "watch out!" As she read it again she wondered whether this dark adult fable was the original pilot of all that improvised childhood entertainment?

<Boomerang's dad never spoke much. He never said hullo or goodbye. He had a favourite chair and if Boomerang sat in it and dad arrived Boomerang needed to scarper fast or get thumped. In the bathroom dad kept a huge leather belt hanging up. Sometimes he would drag Boomerang in there and lash him for no apparent reason. Whenever the cowed little boy asked his mother why his father behaved so meanly she used to shrug and say, "Dad's job is very demanding. His nerves are frayed. And he's anxious a war is going to start."

Boomerang became solitary and withdrawn. He acquired his nickname because he loved to play with the projectile. The huge swirling arc boomerangs made in the sky utterly delighted him. School always oppressed his spirit. He found the teachers stern, pedantic and dry as dog biscuits. He lived only for break times and the release from stuffy classrooms when he could hurl his boomerang across wide-open spaces of sky and field. One day the missile landed on an older boy's head but instead of beating him the older boy returned it with sympathetic curiosity. Over subsequent weeks a playtime relationship developed. Ilario became Boomerang's first real friend, a confidant to whom he could relay all his unspoken feelings of alienation and longing.

"What your mum says about your dad is just a code for something too horrible in their relationship to express," Ilario suggested. "Everything we are taught at home and school and wherever else authority reigns is coded and requires deciphering if the inner truth is to be understood. The school curriculum informs us 1+1 always equals 2 and that the cause of world war one was the assassination of the archduke Franz Ferdinand but in reality that war had multiple diverse causes while 1+1 can equal almost anything! For instance in your mum and dad's case 1+1 adds up to a toxic familial nest of inadequacy, deceit and collusion. Codes are what society uses to programme and regiment us. There are three types of people as follows: 1. Those who learn and internalise the codes so thoroughly they mistake them for articles of unimpeachable reality. 2. Those who perceiving the codes are narrow and flawed conventions work openly to humanise them but fall victim to disappointment, anger or pragmatic self-interest. 3. Those who associate secretly together to create bold new codes of reality while simultaneously protecting themselves from corruption in the process...... How do you know who you are and what you want out of life, Boomerang?"

The boy shook his head. It was a great puzzle. There had to be more to life than waiting for tedious lessons to end and then hurling boomerangs across space. "The truth is," continued Ilario, "the answers to these questions are pressed on you by the codes. You become a reflection of them. Their narrow range of life choices is made to seem the only choices that exist."

Later Boomerang recklessly sought his father out and asked, "Is it because you've never chosen to become what you really yearn to be that you are so angry and miserable?" In return he received a violent beating. Ilario comforted his friend by suggesting that until Boomerang was old enough to leave home he would need to speak to his parents only in the code of childhood innocence and meek filial obligation because it was all they understood.

Subsequently Ilario taught him many things about the relationship between codes and actuality, between meta-representations of the truth and the truth untarnished. For instance when a politician says, "I can imagine no circumstances in which I would ever challenge our leader for the leadership" he really means "Next time our leader fouls up I hope you will nominate me to replace him." And when a priest says in response to a difficult theological question, "The ways of God remain an ineffable mystery" he really means "I'm just as baffled as you by the contradictions of doctrine but I'd be eliminated from the promotion list for bishop if I publicly said so." Ilario also taught Boomerang that the coded ways of the world of experience were derived from a fear of freedom and ferociously guarded.

When Boomerang asked Ilario whether anyone knew the point of humanity he replied, "Do you know why your boomerang keeps coming back when you throw it?" Boomerang pondered that it had something to do with aerodynamics and the forces of nature and his ability to interact with them, an answer that amused Ilario no end. He taught Boomerang that 'the people of the veil', as he called them, develop a sixth sense, a sensitivity to the beautiful interconnectedness and symmetry of organic life, and they signal this ability like moths and birds to attract like-minded others. "They are innocents who have learnt how to survive in the cynical world of adult experience," Ilario explained. Under Ilario's direction Boomerang studied aesthetics, archetypes, cryptology and DNA, in fact all the research indicating the existence of a generative Intelligence within the infrastructure and processes of reality. "People generally filter experience through mental concepts that are ideologically hackneyed and lifeless," Ilario explained. "Switch off the filter even momentarily and another world appears, gloriously rich and breathtakingly unified in elemental meanings, an eternal world."

When the war eventually came it was fought bitterly and lasted seven years. The dead were legion. Ilario had long since disappeared in the conflict. Several months into the uneasy peace Boomerang heard a rumour that Ilario had been imprisoned in an outback detention centre for terrorists. It took many letters before he was granted permission to visit his friend and Boomerang knew it could be a trap. The authorities were vigilantly rounding up fellow travellers. One word out of place and he might be detained indefinitely too. "Your pal is nutty as a fruitcake," the custodial guard taunted Boomerang. "He's been medicated for years. All he does is write crazy poetry. Expect to be dismayed."

And so it proved. Ilario cut a pitiful, emaciated figure. His imbecilic gaze wandered vacantly round the cell. His rambling conversation was not unfriendly but he evidently had no memory of Boomerang or even the school they had once attended. "Would you care to hear me recite some of my poems?" he pleaded childishly. Boomerang pretended to enjoy the garbled nonsense that came spouting out of Ilario's mouth. Had they lobotomised him? Ilario clearly existed merely as the empty shell of his former brilliant self. When he stood up to leave Boomerang felt a scrap of paper being pressed into his hand. "This poem is to thank you for coming," drooled Ilario. "It is called 'One'."

Outside the eves-dropping officers wanted to confiscate the poem but Boomerang objected so they made a photocopy and returned it. Like them when he read it Boomerang judged the lyric to be gobbledygook, vaguely incendiary perhaps in its sentiments but politically harmless:

In auguries my soul awaits nirvana.
Energy becalmed, official opinions murder ecstasy.
Reaction and neurosis garrotte kindness,
Eviscerating equality.
Paupers, take heart!
Endure frost and isolation,
Tomorrow hastens.

And why was it called 'One'? He could detect no relationship between the title and the subject matter. One what? Boomerang slept badly that night back home. 'Endure the frost and isolation' that had descended on the land? How could he? All virtuous opposition to the military government had been crushed. His best friend tortured into a gibbering cretin. Around 3am he made a drink. Ilario's poem lay discarded on the kitchen table and he read it through despondently, One? Why One? he kept asking himself. Then, after twenty minutes just staring, his thinking mind closed down and certain letters gradually began to stand out, to wink at him, as if connected not by grammatical sense but by an invisible electric circuit. Suddenly he saw the scrawl as a child might see an inkblot, as primitive man gazing up at the night sky teeming with thousands of points of light might discern a constellation, an underlying pattern within the chaos.

In **a**uguries **m**y **s**oul **a**waits **n**irvana.
Energy **b**ecalmed, **o**fficial **o**pinions **m**urder **e**cstasy.
Reaction **a**nd **n**eurosis **g**arrotte **k**indness,
Eviscerating **e**quality.

Paupers, **t**ake **h**eart!
Endure **f**rost **a**nd **i**solation,
Tomorrow **h**astens.

The pattern said: **"I am sane, Boomerang. Keep the faith."** Ilario was still there! realised Boomerang as his heart exalted. Ilario's madness was a disguise! And keep the faith Boomerang knew he would until the great freeze ended.>

By mid-day when thick clouds had given way to ragged sunshine Donna decided to stroll down to The London Apprentice, a favourite Sunday watering hole opposite Isleworth Eyot. She enjoyed drawing the wharf and boats where the personality of the river was constantly in flux. And there was always a chance some casual bystander might offer her a commission. Pub prices being prohibitive, at Sarah's prompting, she had stored food and a drink in her artist's satchel. "Why don't you come with me?" suggested Donna. "Unless you've got something else to do?"

"I have actually. I need to do some shopping and I've arranged to see Joc later," reflected Sarah. "But first I want to try and get through another of dad's notebooks. You know Joc has been in California on study leave, don't you? We've got a lot of catching up to do. Don't forget to take your mobile. I'll ring you later. Okay?"

It was not difficult for Donna to find a perch on the embankment wall. The tide had run low and children chased off fat gulls that settled on the pebbly beach. But as she worked Donna found her mind wandering involuntarily back to a television programme she had seen that morning on depression. She still felt tearful and listless since her mother had died but less frequently than she had done six months ago. Time had begun to speed up a bit. When you were bereaved you shouldn't have to go around wearing a brave face, she reckoned, and nobody should expect it of you. The programme reiterated that fact and speculated whether depression should be considered a mood or a disease and whether the condition should be treated with drugs or counselling. A clinician, who worked at a place called The Tavistock, argued that we still lived in "a primitive stiff upper lip, grin and get on with it world that expected us from an early age to suppress all painful emotions." The consequence of this, said the doctor, was an adult population who suffered from a wide range of undiagnosed emotional health problems. "Up to three-quarters of adult mental health problems begin during childhood," he estimated.

Suddenly Donna realised that she had stopped sketching even though her eyes were still fixed intently on the sinewy lime green tresses of the island's trees. What she saw now in the foliage resembled her mother's face and her heart fluttered with delight. A college counsellor had warned Donna not to be frightened by such ghostly visitations – they were a natural consequence of love, he said, and should be treasured. This was by no means the first Donna had experienced. "Life is so long and death is so short," the counsellor had advised her. "There will be many questions but the best answers come from your intuition and imagination and not from your reason. And you, Donna, are very strong in those faculties."

The questions had indeed come thick and fast in the aftermath of bereavement. What sort of life had her mother's really been? And why had it been? What is a human life for, anyway? The last words she remembered her mother saying had helped Donna to survive these questions and the terrible pain of not knowing how to answer them. "I don't want you to fret about me, Donna. I know I'm going to a better place and I'll be making it lovely and comfortable for you and Sarah when you eventually join me." And there had been such a serene conviction in the voice that Donna became imbued with her mother's vision. It sustained her still. Nor did it feel odd to Donna that her mother had never been conventionally religious or anything similar.

Lost in a nostalgic daydream other strands of conversation, other incidents, began to flood through Donna's mind. It was mummy who had encouraged her to keep up her childhood pursuits and value her way of being. "Don't let anyone dictate to you what you need to do," mummy had said once. "Follow your path with a heart. I wanted to be an actress and a long distance runner and an explorer but I allowed myself to be persuaded otherwise and became a mother and travel agent." She had chuckled as she said it, as if making a joke, and it had confused Donna a bit.

"Didn't you want to have children, mummy?" she had asked. "Of course I did!" exclaimed mummy, "And you and Sarah were the greatest adventure of my life." When Donna had been refused admittance to the GCSE Art course on the ground that she was not among the best thirty applicants mummy had gone storming into the school to absolutely demand her daughter's instatement. "Unfortunately your daughter's competent but not quite good enough," apologised the head of Art.

"Good? What does that mean?" retorted mummy. "Good, in the context of a thirteen year old?" Eyebrows were raised. "We have specific criteria – " began the teacher. "Criteria? Really?" mummy had cut in sarcastically. "I have criteria in my hair sometimes. I use a medicated shampoo to get rid of them!" In the end a compromise was negotiated and Donna eventually enrolled on the course. Two years later the "criteria police," as mummy had taken to calling them, awarded her with an A star grade.

Suddenly the ring tone of her mobile phone shifted Donna abruptly back to the present. "You're alright, are you?" demanded a sisterly voice in her ear. Donna felt less than gratified at Sarah's concern. "Well, I haven't fallen in the river, if that's what you mean," she joked back. "Anyway, I'm just off to Richmond now shopping," advised Sarah imperviously, "then I'm going round to Joc's. I'll be back to cook supper about six. Okay?"

Grieving for mummy had hardly become the issue for Sarah that it was for her younger sister. Of course Sarah felt her mother's absence deeply but she did not experience it as an open wound at the very core of her being. Sarah had been psychologically prepared to let her mother go on the journey to wherever the dead went. This had not been true in her father's case. "Death never afflicts you in the same way twice," Joc had counselled. "You don't become callous, that's the wrong word, you become accepting, at the ego level I mean. You live in peace with the ghosts of memory and take comfort from their presence."

For many years guilt and grief combined to haunt Sarah's psyche in a way that neither counselling nor time could mend. "Nothing will heal that wound completely," Joc had observed, "nor should you expect it to. The wound and its related memories is now part of who you are. Such acute pain does not last forever but its ghostly imprints do. You could have been much better advised by your mother and that counsellor man, Williamson, whose influence she fell under – but to transfer blame on to them, rather than to take responsibility for your own developmental issues, is counter-productive. There are many valid reasons for you, indeed for all of us, to be angry about the injustices of life but unless that anger is controlled and directed strategically then it will just keep imploding within your own being and render you perennially unstable."

That had been seven years ago yet today she still felt like someone reborn. The angry, cynical, reckless camouflage of the old Sarah had shrivelled and fallen away and a new self was in charge, a self that knew every true act of rebellion expresses a nostalgia for innocence and an appeal to the essence of being. So now that the obstacle to all the unanswered family questions about the past no longer existed, Sarah had begun to ask them and with Joc's cautious approval. "Just as the death of your father is a part of who you are so is the life you shared together," Joc had advised. "So to reconnect with him should stabilise your sense of identity further - as long as you are prepared for surprises. The father that you discover may not live up to your idealised childhood memories. You must tread carefully."

Jocelyn Merryweather, the daughter of a homophobic Anglican bishop, had spent the majority of her forty-one years treading very carefully through what she jocularly referred to as 'The No-woman's Land of misogyny'. Shortly after 4pm the Unreasonable Club business agenda was dispensed with and the two friends went into catch-up mode. "I've got a date on Wednesday with a bloke called Johnnie," confided Sarah. "He keeps phoning to tell me things about myself he can't possibly have known. Calls it intuition. He's either a brilliant con artist or telepathic. But he's very cagey with it. All I really know about him is that he works as an accountant in East Croydon and reads a lot. Do you reckon some people really have a sixth sense?"

"You ought to meet my aged aunt Alice who won second prize in the national lottery," grinned Joc. "Swears blind she dreamt five of the numbers. We have this family joke now – if you ever find yourself dreaming numbers, don't wake up til you've got all six!" Sarah laughed and Joc added, "Me, I keep an open mind. There are more things in heaven and earth than are dreamt of in your philosophy, Horatio. How's your dad search thing progressing?"

Sarah told Joc about the mysterious arrival of her father's notebooks. She had pestered the courier company who adamantly refused to disclose the contractor. "They're like diaries in part," she explained, "but also full of stories, jokes, and other random scraps of wisdom. Several names keep cropping up. I've written them down in case one or more might mean something to you. Sinclair Scott, Reg Cookson, Martha Bassinger, Richard Weller then just plain Penny and Fina. I've been busy doing google searches. This Weller bloke I actually remember as a pal of dad's and I've seen him recently on the commuter train. But he absolutely denies all knowledge of knowing me or dad."

Joc mulled the list over. "I think there's an actor by the name of Sinclair Scott," she said. "As for the person who sent the journals - perhaps your Dr Williamson's the mystery donor? He might have somehow acquired them through your mother. How did Williamson meet your mum anyway?"

"That's one of the questions I want to ask him," answered Sarah. "I definitely know that mum didn't simply pick his name out of a telephone directory when she decided I needed counselling as a kid. She knew him well before that. He'd been to a couple of social events at our home I remember. There's a photo of him with mum and dad at Donna's christening party - I've let her keep it on the mantelpiece. I'm pretty certain he had once been counselling mum for depression or something and they'd become friends."

"Perhaps the answers to these questions are in the notebooks and that's why he's sent them to you? And perhaps he's hoping they'll get you off his back?" Joc conjectured.

"Maybe," considered Sarah. "But so far I've found nothing really relevant. Williamson's name only crops up twice and in neutral contexts. It's so rude of him to ignore my letters."

"Well if he's dead set his face against talking about your mum and dad you're stumped, I'm afraid," said Joc. "Ring his office again and ask him straight out. At least you will know."

Sarah did more than that. She sent Williamson an email that night and when it remained unanswered by lunchtime the following day she phoned the practice. The woman who took Sarah's call once more refused to connect her. Williamson was working quietly in his room, she explained, after a fraught morning of client consultations. "Fraught?" snarled Sarah ironically. "You tell him I'm coming in tomorrow and I won't be taking 'sorry he's still fraught' for an answer!"

In fact Williamson felt deprived not just of energy but direction and purpose. The previous night he had barely slept a couple of hours and three tediously demanding interviews had now reduced his concentration to tatters. Alas, Edgar Laidlaw, the client who awaited him after lunch, would be even more draining! As he skimmed through the relevant file Williamson reflected on the accumulated weight of his professional experience and how light he might feel once rid of it. Thank God it was Laidlaw's final visit! He shoved the file aside and opened his computer entourage application where another email from Sarah Atkinson lay in wait. *Can you please tell me how you came to know my mother?* one sentence seemed to scream at him and he turned away from the brazen glare of the screen wondering why he couldn't shake off this grim sense of foreboding? It felt as if a vulture was roosting in his abdomen and waiting for him to die. Perhaps the grim reaper had swung a scythe in his direction and the vortex of mortality had drained almost to the dregs? In *Heaven And Earth,* he recalled, the author opined that, "The physical process of dying begins immediately a person believes he has nothing left to live for. Time seizes hold of him like a tourniquet," and the sentences had chilled his blood. For a while he tried to read but within seconds the analyst relaxed back involuntarily on the patient couch and closed his eyes. He felt the blackness swallow his being like an executioner's hood then waited calmly as if for the final spasm of pain before the plunge into oblivion.

DREAM AND REALITY

 Suddenly he seemed to be floating upright down a luminescent tunnel. Occasionally someone would drift past him as if returning the other way. Eventually the tunnel divided and the light dramatically intensified blinding him as he veered along the left fork. When he dared to reopen his eyes the journey had ended and a clinical reception annex confronted his gaze. An electronic device instructed him to confirm his gender and date of birth. He keyed in the relevant digits and the welcoming words appeared, *Thank you, Martin Williamson. Please take a seat.*

A poster opposite declared, *The market is not the guarantor of human happiness and never will be.* He looked to his right and a second notice advised, *As fish unwittingly inhabit the seas, so humanity unwittingly inhabits power.* He turned his head back to the first notice but a man stood in front of it, dressed in a sky blue suit with a pink cravat. A lapel badge advertised the name, Edgar. "Hullo," smiled Edgar ethereally. "Will you please follow me?"

The corridor they entered smelled of pine disinfectant and vomit. Another poster announced, *The facts do not really exist until Value has created them. If your own values are rigid you cannot learn new facts.* Then Edgar ushered him into a room and closed the door. An embankment of switches and monitors occupied most of the space. Several drably naturalistic movies were in progress. "Where am I exactly?" asked Williamson sinking at Edgar's request into a leather swivel chair. "Don't I know you?"

"You are on the first astral plain," answered Edgar ignoring the other question. "It is my job to supervise a detailed review of your life. Once we have established you have learnt from your mistakes then you will be permitted to move on to the second."

"How many plains are there?" asked Williamson, his eyes flickering between the active monitors and Edgar's increasingly familiar face.

"Seven," replied Edgar. "Haven't you heard of Seventh Heaven?"

"I thought it was just a figure of speech," smirked Williamson. "So this dump is Heaven, is it?"

"This is the karmic assessment centre, Martin," corrected Edgar. "Perhaps you would prefer I defer to your earthly status and call you Dr Williamson?"

"Whatever," shrugged Williamson. "So I'm in Purgatory then? If I fail your bloody test I slide down some chute into Hell?"

This induced the ghost of a smile to form on Edgar's fulsome lips. "It still amazes me how the human mind conjures up such apocalyptic anxieties," he said. "Hell is not a physical location. It is the ego's hostile response to other people."

Williamson screwed up his face and moaned, "It's not my fault. I didn't ask to be born!"

"Oh dear, we get that a lot," sighed the lifetime assessor. "Especially from brutal dictators and mass murderers. I hadn't expected it from an erudite humanist psychotherapist." He opened a file and skimmed through it, saying, "You were born in Lancashire after the war, the somewhat timid over-protected child of Michael and Doris. After a routinely mediocre university career you went into marketing, married then separated after nine months. Two further romantic relationships failed. Ah, then you found a niche in East London teaching angry teenagers too disruptive to be kept in ordinary schools. You are good at it, no question, but the job is very stressful and so in your mid thirties you retrain to become a psychoanalyst specialising initially in adolescent problems."

At this rate of knots the review will be over in ten minutes and I'll be in second heaven, thought Williamson.

"No you won't," retorted Edgar telepathically. "Time is the encumbrance of mortality. It has no existence in this dimension."

"Who's that young woman," said Williamson pointing at one of the monitors. "I seem to recognise her. What's going on?"

Edgar blanked all the screens with a flick of his remote and replied, "These show only real time events, things happening right now. But it is the Atkinson family on which I want to historically focus. As you know Margaret, the mother, expired quite recently from an incurable cancer. Don, the father, died in a road accident some 18 of your years ago." He paused as if expecting his guest to elaborate. "I suppose you don't precisely recall how you met Margaret?"

"I bumped into her on a station platform," Williamson answered. "Saturday October 17, 1986, the week of the great storm. Is that precise enough for you?" Edgar activated a large plasma screen and images of fallen trees and power lines appeared, quickly dissolving to a domestic kitchen where a man Williamson recognised as Don Atkinson stood preparing a meal. "You think I'm in denial about something, do you?" demanded Williamson.

"Even a shrink can be in denial sometimes," observed Edgar and commenced narrating. "Don was cooking the evening meal when Margaret arrived home about 6.30. He offered her a token brush of the cheek before casually saying, 'Can I speak to you about something important?' Margaret responded with a shudder of anxiety. At that moment little Sarah ran in joyously from the bedroom. 'I've been having a relationship with Grace,' Don admitted later when they were safely alone. 'We've been....you know.....' The telling word failed him. He averted his gaze to the remote tundra of the carpet.

"'For how long?' Margaret heard herself ask almost politely.

"'Let me see? A year, maybe,' Don reflected. 'I've finished it, of course. And I'm really very sorry I haven't told you before. I've meant to for ages. I've been so weak. So cowardly.' Synthetic tears began to form in his eyes.

"Margaret felt like an embarrassed evesdropper on someone else's drama. Part of her had retreated to the ceiling for refuge and was gazing down at the prim, stiff stranger who sat on the sofa wearing the offended woman's clothes. Grace was her best friend! 'How did this relationship start?' the stranger asked eventually.

"'I was performing at a pub in Islington one night,' Don explained contritely, 'and Grace turned up to see the show. She invited me back to her place for a drink and one thing, I suppose, led to another. Look, Margaret, I can't tell you how mortified I feel about it!'

"It took another 24 hours for the news to sink in properly. When they went to bed that night Don reached out to caress his wife but Margaret shrugged him off and rolled to the edge of the mattress. The numbness, the out of body sensation, persisted right through the following day. Often Margaret commuted to work by public transport but that Tuesday she seized the family car and threaded her way through the dense rush hour traffic almost as an act of penance, dropping Sarah off at her nursery en route. How had she failed Don? That was the question uppermost in her mind all day. When she arrived back home with Sarah, Don already had the table laid, a bottle of wine opened, and was behaving in an impeccably solicitous manner.

"As they ate it did occur to Margaret that she ought to be demonstrably upset, that this display of self-control demeaned her. She may have remained immobilised like that for weeks, too, but about 8.30 the phone rang. After about five minutes Don entered the bathroom apologetically and tense. 'I'm sorry to disturb you while you're in the bath,' he began, 'but Grace is on the phone. She desperately wants to talk to you.'

"'Tell her to get lost!' snapped Margaret. 'She wants to apologise and explain,' objected Don. 'She sounds distraught.' In a flash Margaret had thrown the soap at him then the shampoo bottle, then Sarah's plastic hippo plus anything else that came to hand. Water spilled over onto the floor in spasms of fury. 'Tell her never to phone here again! I'm finished with the bitch!'

"In bed that night she found it difficult to settle into sleep. On the occasions she managed to doze off her dreams were haunted with all manner of strange, bloodsucking creatures that leeched on to her arms and breasts and face. About 3am she switched on the bedside lamp and studied the incubus lying there next to her, slumbering like a baby without a care in the world. Its face, puffy with excess alcohol, looked simultaneously happy and moronic against the pillow-spread. The duvet had become partially displaced from the body and she grimaced to see the skinny, undeveloped arms and hairy buttocks. They made her feel suddenly nauseous and disgusted. Although the creature displayed recognisably masculine characteristics, Margaret experienced its presence in her psyche as a slimy, parasitic intruder – a garden slug that has somehow managed to slither through a tiny crevice into her heart's affections and set up home there, defiling all it touches. How could she ever have allowed this to happen? She levered herself out of bed and padded noiselessly towards the sanctity of the door. Don's underpants and sweaty socks had been dropped like toxic debris on the floor and she flicked them distastefully out of her way with her toes. Why should he be able to lie in her bed and sleep? He was an eyesore, a health hazard. Clumps of hair sprouted out of his ears and nostrils. Everything about the careless lack of regard for his basic hygiene was hideous. Why should she allow him to remain in the flat, let alone her bedroom?

"The next morning after she had secured Sarah in the car she briefly returned to the maisonette and snarled, 'I don't want you here when I come home. Understand? Pack up and clear off!'- "

"Enough!" shouted Williamson and banged his fist on a red button. Amazingly it worked. The screen image of Margaret froze, the narrator hiccoughed to a halt and Williamson darted frantically for the escape door.

 For Martin Williamson scurrying desperately up and down the labyrinthine corridors of the karmic assessment centre there was no way out. Behind every door he opened stood the lifetime assessor smiling benignly. Edgar was evidently ubiquitous. After several futile escape attempts the psychoanalyst surrendered to his fate. "I became inappropriately attached to her," he confessed slumping into a chair, "to Margaret, my patient. That was unforgivably unprofessional."

"Not a sliver as unprofessional as your subsequent plot against her husband," taunted Edgar.

It occurred to Williamson to interject that when a mortal suffers chronic pain, for whatever cause, time slows down. Time crawls with immeasurable tedium from moment to agonising moment and what was previously experienced as normality is hideously distorted and misunderstood. Innocence is blighted, the acts of angels seem demonic and every virtuous impulse is sublimated beneath the basic instinct to survive. But he held his counsel and slowly raised his eyes to the TV monitor where the woman he had once illicitly loved with an inordinate passion placed a kitchen knife in her handbag then strode out into the wilderness of storm ravaged London to seek and dispatch her oldest friend, Grace.

"It was now Saturday," narrated Edgar. "Don was lodging with his pal, Reg, obedient to Margaret's wishes, and taken Sarah with him. So how should we understand this gentle-natured woman's sudden murderous resolve?"

"As a form of temporary insanity," opined Williamson reluctantly. "Grace had been Margaret's closest friend from early childhood. Between men, emotionally inhibited as they are conditioned to be, friendship is always pragmatic and disposable. Between women friendship can be as vitally important as oxygen. The decision to kill Grace had not arrived as an idea in Margaret's sensibility so much as an impregnation in her body. At a certain moment she had become fecund with hatred. Somewhere in her womb a foetus had gestated, an alien entity that did not belong to her and was reproducing cancerous secondary growths in random sinews and tissue. Grace had placed it there and Margaret felt that she would have neither peace of mind nor purpose of life ever again until the monster was aborted."

"Indeed," concurred Edgar. "Vindictive voices thundered in Margaret's head as she strode mechanically towards the embankment until a forensically cold thought separated itself from the cacophony and admonished her strategic naivety. 'Circumstances require you to be devious as well as ruthless,' it announced to her. 'Grace lives in a house with three other employees of the bank. How are you going to isolate her?'

"She jumped on a bus only to disembark forty minutes later when it stalled in a gridlocked diversion. Spotting a red phone kiosk she experienced a brief moment of lucidity and dialled 999. 'Please, I need help – urgently. I – I – I'm about to commit a mu – murder,' she stammered.

"A hiatus followed, an interminable silence during which Margaret caught sight of her eyes in a surface reflection of cracked mirror. They leered back at her, abominably wide and demented. 'Is this a hoax call?' sneered the operator and Margaret dropped the receiver with sudden disgust as if it was contaminated."

Edgar fast-forwarded again. In eerily silent quick time Williamson watched Margaret enter a taxi. It sped across London to Islington where she paid the fare then furrowed on foot through dank litter strewn streets.

"An odour of refuse and rotting vegetables assaulted her nostrils," continued Edgar. "The people who passed her were like shadows, the inhabitants of another dimension, and when she arrived at the Victorian terraced house where Grace lived, it too stood outside space-time like a mausoleum in a dimly remembered dream. Eventually a couple emerged and shuffled away hand in hand, blind to her palpitating, hawkeyed presence.

"And so Margaret kept vigil, periodically pacing up and down the street and exploring the variegated nooks and crannies it offered as espionage points. A middle-aged man came and went, then came again, a roll-up dangling from his mouth, his jowly, alcohol-sodden face bristling several days growth of beard. Out of the corner of her eyes she measured his approaching tottery gait. He pulled a wad of banknotes out of his pocket, belched obscenely and flourished them with a gesture of unambiguous intent. Suddenly fifty yards beyond his shoulder Margaret saw the door open again and Grace appeared. Grace looked nonchalantly towards them, a brief untroubled glance, and instantly marched off in the opposite direction, swinging a patchwork wooden-handled emerald bag that matched her jacket. Margaret knew she had not been recognised. The drunk was making a lewd proposition but she dismissed it with a snort of derision and he cursed her and floundered on his way.

"As she followed her prey at a safe distance Margaret remembered the kitchen knife. Speed and precision would be essential, she thought. But what if Grace turned and the first thrust missed the jugular? Suddenly Grace stopped outside a shop. Her eyes seemed to be transfixed on a window display of advertisements.

"I could do it now, thought Margaret opening her handbag and clutching the knife secreted within. A woman pushing a pram emerged from the shop door and turned almost suspiciously, Margaret thought, towards her. Then a car pulled up, a man alighted and entered the premises. Margaret had inched within twenty yards of her target but still she hesitated. All she needed to do was sprint forward and plunge the knife down hard and clean into the nape of that unsuspecting neck yet even as she articulated the resolution in her mind Grace turned and walked briskly away with a flagrant disregard for her assassin that seemed almost telepathic. Never mind, nothing is lost, the stalker told herself as she pursued Grace along teeming pavements, across gridlocked road junctions. She was growing in confidence. With patience and focus the right opportunity to strike was bound to appear.

"If the automaton that Margaret had become could be said to have revised its intention about the execution of a strategic plan – it occurred within moments of Grace entering The Angel underground station. She watched her quarry insert coins into a ticket machine and discreetly followed suit at another dispenser. A small crowd straggled around the alcove waiting for an access lift to arrive and Margaret slipped inconspicuously into its midst as they mustered like eager troops into the compressed oblong space. Grace headed for the southbound walkway as she alighted. The main bulk of travellers had assembled at a mid-section of the platform but Grace threaded her way through them towards the inlet mouth of the tunnel. Margaret could tell from the assurance with which Grace manoeuvred herself that she knew the geography of the place by second nature. She knew the exact place the waiting crowd dissipated, the exact spot to stand in order to be opposite a train door. She knew how close to the edge to safely locate. Grace was totally self-contained and cocooned in the act of waiting as only habitual frequenters of the tube can be, staring in a trance towards the gaping black hole from which in two minutes, according to the electronic sign, the next southbound train would emerge in a great rush of wind and litter, and crush her to extinction.

"Margaret produced a handkerchief and pretended to be using it to treat some nasal problem as she edged undetected into position several feet behind her friend. She was by now, in her own crazed estimation of things, an entirely invisible agent of requital. Insofar as she belonged to the tangible world at all, it was purely to the remorseless abstraction of justice and retribution. The digit on the electronic sign blinked down to one minute. In the corner of her right eye a man appeared lugging a bulky suitcase but fortunately stopped three yards short of her position. That was still an impediment, Margaret considered. He would see it all – the push, the flailing arms and legs, the crunch and splatter of bones against steel and he would hear the scream of terror echoing in his memory for many years – but with any luck he would be too shocked to register the sequence and cause of events or recognise their executor as she escaped rapidly into the exit corridor.

"Somewhere far away in the bowels of the earth the ominous throb of a burrowing animal suddenly asserted itself, eclipsing every filigree of distraction. Grace seemed to yawn and shift laconically from one foot to another. Move closer to the edge, Margaret mentally urged her victim and the wish became magically granted. The throb transposed into a roar, surging now like a tidal wave about to hit the shore, a subterranean drill bursting through the fissures of the Earth's crust and breaking the surface. Hold your position, Margaret instructed herself. Hold your position! The timing of the lunge would need to be perfect. And now the luminous eyes of the beast came into view, the obscene head of the serpent writhing out of its hideous burrow. Closer. Louder. The pilot suddenly etched like a tattoo between the staring sockets, rigid, unsuspecting. This is it, Margaret told herself and launched herself forward with outstretched arms at the target."

Williamson turned away from the obscenity of the screen, his thoughts consumed by the bizarre coincidences and meetings that must characterise every human life, not just his own. It momentarily struck him how primitive a tool Reason is with which to decipher the improbable riddle of heaven and earth.

"Margaret lay on the platform, dazed and unsure what had happened," continued Edgar. "It may have been the interloper's shoulder she had hit, it may have been his midriff and thighs. Then there was his massive bulging suitcase. Her feet had become entangled in the apparatus as she rebounded off the moving obstacle as it appeared suddenly out of nowhere impeding the attack on Grace. He was peering down at her spread-eagled indignity, scowling indignation and blocking her view of the train as it squealed to a halt. 'What were you doing?' he demanded. 'Didn't you see me?' Behind him the train doors slid open and the interchange of passengers began. The man bent down to her now – you, Martin, please look - and you held out a hand. She tried to grasp it but missed. 'Take your time. You may have jarred your back,' you said much more sympathetically. 'I'm a heavy bloke and that was quite a collision.'

"Grace? Margaret thought to herself. Where is she? Then the doors whooshed shut in response and the train pulled away, evidently with Grace on it. 'I've made you miss your train,' Margaret stuttered. And as you helped her onto a bench and ministered to her bruises she saw herself as if from a vast height, cold and outcast, a deranged waif adrift in the universe."

Don't we all? thought Williamson bitterly as Edgar froze the frame and invited his subject to continue the story. "I assumed she'd been attempting suicide," he said. "There were jumpers almost every week back then. I took her under my wing, accompanied her to her home station and gave her my professional card and encouraged her to ring me. A few days later she did. Every Saturday morning she came for counselling until the following May."

"I don't intend to revisit all those counselling sessions," smiled Edgar thinly. "Perhaps you could just summarise your contribution to Margaret's recovery?"

Williamson shook his head. "Modesty forbids," he muttered. "You watch the film while I take a nap." And he tried to close his eyes but found the lids would not budge.

Edgar ran the tape fast forward, intermittently stopping and monitoring his subject's gasps and moans. One question pointedly followed another. "You went a few times to the Atkinson flat and met Don and some of his friends, didn't you?" No reply. "You thought Don was a swollen headed minor celebrity who remained a compulsive philanderer?" Silence. "You considered Margaret far too good for him? You couldn't believe it when she told you she had decided to forgive Don and move on in the relationship?" Still no answers. "Can you recall how surprised you felt when Margaret told you she was expecting another baby by Don?"

This loosened Williamson's reticent tongue. "It is by no means established that Don was the father of that child," he grimaced.

"She was christened Donna in honour of her father," asserted Edgar playing scenes from the christening party. They showed Williamson in attendance. From there Edgar cut to a location in a smoke filled room where three drunken men that included Williamson sat conspiring about something. The psychoanalyst yelped in panic and hit the red stop button. Edgar shoved his face up close and asked, "So let's talk about this green eyed monster of jealousy that began to eviscerate you, Martin?"

"You tell me something first," retorted Williamson fiercely. "Is this God who judges me, through a simpering sanctimonious freak like you, jealous of the human race, having given us free will and then found he cannot control us? Did he create mankind in order to torture him with uncertainty and infirmity and old age? What is your God's intention in making us so passionate and vulnerable, such prey to the ephemeral?"

"You will discover the answer to these questions when you enter the seventh astral plane," simpered Edgar. "Correction. The questions will simply cease to exist. Your awareness will become expanded to a place where everything is pure answer and you are part of that answer."

"For numerous reasons that doesn't make intellectual sense," complained Williamson. "I may never attain your Seventh Heaven, anyway!"

"Not while you continue with your cold cerebral pursuit of reality," scolded Edgar. "As you were correctly speculating just a few minutes ago the intellect is merely an analytical machine invented and subsequently deified by post Enlightenment scientific man for carving reality into pieces and keeping them at a safe distance from his deepest intuitions."

"Get out of my head! I despise your mystical semantics!" barked Williamson. "I despise your Nobodaddy boss! God's only excuse is He does not exist! When I died I expected, nay, welcomed Oblivion, and what I've received instead is this infernally hypocritical interrogation of my motives!" Williamson stood up, apoplectic with anger. "Well, the game is up. You want to hurl me down the chute into some bottomless pit then get on with it. I withdraw all cooperation!"

It took a second for him to reach the corridor. "There must be an ending to the passage," he thought as he fled. "There is always an ending."

"Dr Williamson?" he heard echoing remotely in his wake. "Dr Williamson?" But the psychoanalyst did not look back. He simply quickened his pace. Still the caller persisted and appeared to be drawing closer to the exit when the floor gave way and he entered a state of free fall. "What happened?" he gasped as he landed with a thud of pain. "Where am I?"

The anxious face of the medical partnership's receptionist appeared to be looming over him. Was she dead too? "I'm sorry, I didn't realise you were asleep on the couch," Silvia apologised. "I didn't intend to make you fall off, only your two o'clock appointment is waiting outside a bit impatiently, Edgar Laidlaw."

Williamson's face exuded incomprehension as he mouthed the name again. "Yes, you know," said Silvia, "The university don who speaks in aphorisms all the time. Look, you left his case notes file open on the floor and a book."

Williamson gazed around in relief. He was back in the land of what was professionally assumed to be the living. "I must have been reading them," he muttered. Silvia handed him his splayed copy of *Heaven And Earth* open at a chapter discussing theories of the afterlife. It had evidently dropped to the floor with him. She busied herself tidying around the room, collecting a plate of sandwich crumbs amongst other things. "You look a bit crumpled," she remarked. "I'll make an excuse to Mr Laidlaw while you freshen up, shall I?"

Certainly Williamson felt groggy on his feet. "I've been sleeping so badly at night," he explained, "ever since, well, never mind."

"Oh, by the way, that Atkinson woman has been on the phone yet again," said the receptionist. "Most aggressive in her manner. If you don't get back to her, she implied, she intends to turn up here and cause a row. I didn't like her attitude one bit."

Williamson recalled now Sarah's letters and follow up emails. The most recent was still open on his computer screen, having arrived as he began to eat his lunch. *From: Sarah Atkinson*, it announced. *Subject: My mother and father.* As he threw water on his face in the bathroom the analyst noticed his hands were shaking with trepidation.

Five minutes later when Edgar was ushered into the consultancy room Williamson found himself trying to avoid meeting the client's eyes. Edgar had apparently left his natty blue suit and pink cravat back at the karmic assessment centre and was now sporting black corduroys and grey windjammer in addition to a supercilious swagger. "Sorry to keep you waiting," the analyst muttered offering a seat. "I believe this is our last meeting. So where do you wish to begin, er, Mr Laidlaw?"

Edgar stared back at him for a long time with brazen condescension just as he had in real life. But this is real life, isn't it, surely? Williamson questioned himself. Suddenly the client broke the silence. "How about with madness?" he grinned. The analyst raised a nervous eyebrow. "I heard that Barbara Martelli woman on the radio this morning comparing madness to influenza," continued Edgar. "Anyone can catch it and there's no immunity. There are hundreds of different viruses floating in the psycho-social atmosphere and they're constantly mutating."

"I suppose there's some truth in that," replied Williamson garnering his professional manner as best he could. "Does the proposition worry you then?"

"Me? Worry me?" mocked Edgar raising his nose to a superior height. "Why of course not! It's you I'm concerned for, Mr Williamson. Your ashen face tells me you are in the grip of some demented lurgy."

SANITY AND MADNESS

 A copy of The Guardian newspaper rested as yet unread on Johnnie Woo's desk where he had been seated for several hours assiduously preparing the tax returns of a firm of shoemakers called Fletcher Brothers. Weller had rung in shortly after 9.30am to explain he had been 'unavoidably delayed' and Johnnie pretended to acquiesce. No other option was open to him. Weller might have a legitimate business meeting, but more than likely he had just gone off on a bender or to the races or found some nubile female company. The euphemism 'unavoidably delayed' was a catchall, covering a plethora of possibilities, most of them sinful. Not that this executive indolence bothered Johnnie's routine. Indeed Weller's absences from the office in East Croydon nowadays increasingly came as a relief. He made coffee and located the radio four stream on his computer. A programme called *All In The Mind* was about to be broadcast and he could enjoy it in peace. Today's edition would be looking at the work

done by an organisation called *Sanity Matters* whose purpose was to challenge the stigmas and negative attitudes that are still widely associated with mental health, learning disability and addiction, and it would feature an interview with Barbara Martelli, one of its founding members.

Could this Martelli woman be prevailed upon to help him make sense of his own nonsensical deviant life? Johnnie had long been wondering. Could she reassure him that this extraordinary sensitivity and telepathic intuition he had recently developed was not symptomatic of incipient lunacy – because that was how it often felt to him. The programme presenter introduced his studio guest and said, "In your latest book, *Heaven And Earth*, you make the contentious assertion that nearly all of us go mad at least once in our life time. Can you explain a bit what you mean by that and your own personal family experiences of the madness state?" And Johnnie was instantly all ears.

"Yes, well my point is that we are all capable of going off the rails if our life becomes unbearably stressful," Martelli replied. "Fortunately most of us recover after relatively short therapy, for others it may take much longer. Of course, I refer to the madness that has its causality not in some disease of the biological organism but in the pressures of everyday experience. As Lucy Johnstone indicates, 'There is now conclusive evidence that most people break down as a result of a complex mix of social and psychological circumstances – bereavement and loss, poverty and discrimination, trauma and abuse, even love and rejection'.

"Abuse during childhood is one of the major causes of adult psychosis. I went mad for a time when I was a teenager. Aged sixteen I fell passionately in love with a man much older than me and became pregnant. My mortified parents took the baby away a few days after her birth and had her adopted while my lover was paid off handsomely to disappear - abuses for which I still bear residual emotional scars today. However my parents did have the sense subsequently to send me for counselling. Thwarted desire, jealousy, low self-esteem, pride, anger can all be the agents of festering lunacy, especially if kept secret and untreated. Their archetypes abound in our greatest literature.

Oedipus, King Lear, Miss Havisham, the Macbeths, Captain Ahab, Hamlet, Clytemnestra, Othello. The hold those characters retain over the human imagination is no coincidence.

"When my adopted daughter was 20 she came looking for me and we were reconciled. She had fallen in love with a lovely talented man who turned out, as the result of childhood abuse, to be secretly confused about his sexual orientation. His only previous romantic attachment had been to a man. He feared analysis, the stigma of being branded abnormal, and it was only several years later when his marriage to another woman was threatening to disintegrate that he undertook therapy. Very few of us do not suffer similar such dilemmas of identity at some period during our lives. If the dilemma is not confronted it is invariably pushed into our unconscious mind and we become thereby split in two. We act duplicitously without knowing it. And such splitting of the personality is far more common than we are generally prepared to recognise."

Suddenly the phone rang and Johnnie killed the radio sound as he answered. "Richard Weller

Accounts. Johnnie Woo speaking," he said. "Can I help you?" It was one of the Fletchers wanting to discuss their tax returns. This would not be quick unfortunately. *All In The Mind* would just have to wait for another time.

Eight miles due north as the hypothetical crow flies Martin Williamson, having sufficiently recovered from his dual encounters with Edgar Laidlaw and enjoyed a better night's sleep, was also wrestling with the problem of sanity and madness. It was not contractually necessary for the therapist to send a discharge report to the client's vice-chancellor but the request had been made. Whatever he wrote would not regain Laidlaw his academic post, that much was clear, but it might ensure an unblemished reference from the university should Laidlaw decide to seek similar employment elsewhere. The salient questions were as follows: 'Did the client have a mental health problem? Had the client demonstrated a willingness to understand and control his angry impulses?' A psychiatrist might easily have diagnosed the client as bi-polar or suffering from a borderline personality disorder and prescribed an appropriate mood altering drug but he, Williamson, was a clinical psychologist and trained to believe that every life, however badly knotted its history had become, could eventually be untangled.

For all his fierce in your face credos and irony Laidlaw had occasionally betrayed a startlingly childlike naivety and vulnerability. At the previous day's final consultation, for instance, he had narrated a baroque story about an American entrepreneur called Luke Karamba. This Karamba was, Williamson knew, merely an opportunistic hustler with a huge organisation of clones who had recently flooded the streets and cyberspace flogging get-rich-quick schemes to the gullible. Yet Laidlaw had been somehow tricked into handing over his contact details and for the last fortnight had been bombarded with emails, as many as twelve each day, pressurising him to invest in one dodgy business scheme or another. "It's driving me potty," Laidlaw had pleaded to his analyst. "It's such a vulgar and despicable assault on one's privacy!" When Williamson had suggested all he needed to do was change the junk filter to 'high' to prevent the sales pitches from appearing on the screen the client wept with joyful gratitude. The unworldly don had not been aware of the existence of any such computer application!

Gradually over the months, therefore, a picture of not one but two distinct Edgar Laidlaws had emerged for the analyst - the public and the private, the arrogant aesthete and the insecure loner, the visionary crusader and the frightened child. The strain of managing these two selves appeared to have created in the client unresolved tensions of anger, resentment, narcissism, obsessive compulsiveness and judgementalism. In his notes Williamson had observed, "The man is a ticking time bomb of contradictions who refuses so far to be un-detonated." But this was hardly an insight that could be advantageously shared with the vice-chancellor. It was a truth too far for comfort. *The* man? *All* men? *The human race?* Where on earth did this observation not have a general application? Williamson stood up and walked wearily to the window. A sudden change in the weather had welded the city into a grey amorphous canopy of drizzle. This bloody job is doing my head in, he thought. Perhaps I ought to take that retirement deal after all while it's still on the table?

Sarah Atkinson on her way to rendezvous with Jocelyn had again been accosted by one of Karamba's smarmy salesmen, this time on the precinct outside the National Theatre, but she had given him short shrift. "Good morning, Miss!" he had called. "And what a lovely day it is to commit to becoming filthy rich. Can I interest you in - ?" Sarah had simply gestured towards the imminent rain clouds and given a one-fingered salute.

"These Karamba hustlers are one of the plagues of neo-liberalism. Even the weather doesn't deter them. They're breeding faster than rats all over the city," said Jocelyn as the two women ate lunch in the Olivier cafeteria. Joc was there to see the matinee of a Caryl Churchill revival. "I've had them in my face three times this week. By the way, take a look at this ad in The Metro. Barbara Martelli is doing a talk soon for the North London Women Writers' Cooperative about the disconnection between feeling and reason. Do you fancy going?"

Sarah read it and said, "Looks interesting but I'm teaching that night unfortunately. By the way, I've got a lead on that actor bloke Sinclair

Scott. I've spoken to his agent and I've found out that Martha Bassinger is a telly producer," she confided. "And after we've eaten I'm going to barge in on Williamson. His office is only a few hundred yards from here."

Joc opened The Guardian at an article she had just been reading and suggested they might use it as a discussion document at their next full meeting of The Unreasonable Club. *DUPED AND TRAFFICKED* read the headline. Underneath a sub-heading explained, *More and more women are being trafficked from abroad into prostitution, with the UK considered fertile ground. Our reporter Jeremy Blythe talks to victims and asks 'who are the underworld vice kings?'*

Over his own solitary sandwich lunch Johnnie Woo had read the same report with considerable trepidation. He located it on the newspaper website and emailed the link to Weller with a cautionary message saying, *Could this article become the political incentive to a new vice squad initiative?* For months now he had wanted out of the vice trafficking game but feared wrathful consequences. As he poured another coffee from the percolator and stared into its murky depths Johnnie's sordid past came searing shamefully back into his mind's eye.

Brought up in an orphanage he had eventually run away and become a street urchin, living from hand to mouth, hanging around tourist hotels pimping and procuring. "You like a nice lady, mister?" had been the first words he spoke to Richard Weller. It was to be the beginning of a mutually rewarding relationship. The Englishman had recognised in the youngster a shrewdness, ambition and business acumen that, although embryonic, certainly matched his own. Johnnie was lifted out of the Hong Kong gutter, nurtured and educated. The two became loyal partners in what neither man chose to recognise as crime. "Sex without love is a meaningless activity," Weller had once declared to Johnnie, "but as far as meaningless activities go it's still pretty damn good - and the market opportunities for selling it are unlimited." Much later when Johnnie had fallen ill with testicular cancer Weller had taken him to the USA to be treated by the very best oncologists and he had recovered. Johnnie owed his boss and patron big time, therefore. What on earth did he do? He needed to talk to someone absolutely honestly about his predicament. He needed moral support and not for the first time in recent days he thought of Sarah. Could she be that friend he needed? After a couple of meetings he had felt a close affinity with her. She was intelligent and forthright and easy to talk to but - ? There was an enormous one of those. Any honest confession might utterly disgust her and render their burgeoning relationship stone dead. She might even shop him to the police. What did he do next? Who could he trust for help?

 Williamson looked up from his computer. He could hear two voices animated by anger. Outside in the reception area an argument seemed to be in progress. He opened the door and saw Silvia on her feet saying, "I regard this intrusion as a breach of security and unless you leave right now I shall phone the police." The woman to whom these words were addressed had her back to him. "Can I be of assistance?" he butted in. As the intruder turned to face him he felt a mordant pang of recognition. Sarah had grown up to become the mirror image of her mother.

Once she was seated in the privacy of Williamson's office Sarah apologised for her abrasiveness but the analyst waved it away and offered an apology of his own. He had been abroad when Margaret died and deeply regretted missing the funeral. The last time he had spoken with her the cancer had been in remission. Sarah thanked him for his condolences and remarked, "My mother was a stoic. I know she was your client before she made me become yours. Can you tell me what she consulted you about, please?"

The analyst regretted that he was bound by the ethics of confidentiality and could not disclose the content of their meetings. "I see," smiled Sarah. "Did you have an affair with my mother?" she asked in retaliation.

"No, of course not," came the almost indignant reply. "Why do you ask that?"

"Because she had a lot of boyfriends after dad died. None of them ever stuck for long," said Sarah. "I got to imagining you must have been one of them. Carl Jung used to screw his female patients, after all, and you are a Jungian psychologist I understand?" Williamson did not rise to the bait. "Why didn't you reply to my letters and emails?" she persisted further.

"Forgive me for saying this, Sarah, but do you think it's healthy for you to be probing around in your parents' lives?" answered Williamson. "The past is the past. There's only so much scar tissue you can pick off the corpse. I'd like you to consider the following proposition. You are an orphan, albeit a grown-up one, but being suddenly parentless must necessarily involve a radical period of psychological adjustment for you. You will still be numb and very much grieving for both your parents but especially for your mother. And this sudden obsession with the past is an unconscious way of expressing that grief which may simply cause you much more pain."

"Ah, the unconscious!" exclaimed Sarah. "I wondered if that particular monster was going to raise its ugly head." She opened her bag and extracted the notebook she had brought with her while all the time keeping her eyes fixed on Williamson's face as she passed it to him.

"What's this?" he asked inscrutably.

"You don't know?"

"No. Should I?"

"There's a cardboard page marker inside," directed Sarah. "If you go to that page and check out the paragraph I've coloured in yellow all will be revealed."

Williamson quickly found the page and read silently as follows: *Psychotherapy is constructed on the assumption that normality in terms of human behaviour can be specifically identified and even quantified, that there are, for example, gradations of madness and depression. To be madly in love is normal. To be mad with rage, however, is not. It is an aberration. To be chronically depressed because your family have been killed in a terrorist attack is normal. To be chronically depressed because only 4% of men accused of raping women are ever prosecuted by the police, is, however, abnormal.* "Is this your notebook?" asked Williamson looking up from the page with undisguised distaste.

"It is now. It belonged to my dad," replied Sarah triumphantly, "and there's another eleven like it."

"I see. And this material pertains to what – one of his stand up comedy routines?"

"I'd say he was writing in earnest. I can't detect a joke in that paragraph anywhere," smiled

Sarah. "These notebooks only turned up anonymously in the post recently. You were my prime suspect as the donor but I'm obviously wrong. Have you got any idea who might have been in secret possession of my dad's notebooks for all these years?"

Williamson shook his head and handed the journal back. "Sorry. Look, I've got a consultation now, Sarah. Is there anything else?"

"I don't know," answered Sarah holding her ground. "You tell me."

Richard Weller had good reason to be concerned about his protégé and business partner. In recent months an air of detachment and brooding introspection had descended on Johnnie Woo. It was in Johnnie's nature to be cautious, Weller knew, but this flagging up of The Guardian article as if it was an unexploded bomb waiting to be trodden on pointed beyond professional wariness to a deeper malaise. It was but a short stroll from East Croydon station to the office block and as he opened the front door, emblazoned with the gilt company logo, *R.C.WELLER ASSOCIATES – ACCOUNTANTS*, the familiar voice of a woman accosted his ears. Weller padded noiselessly towards the inner door, slightly ajar, guarding the room in which he knew Johnnie would be busy working on The Fletcher Brothers account and stood outside listening.

"Let me deal with your question about love first," he heard. "Of course there is no such thing as unconditional love. It's a romantic myth, perhaps a Christian one too. Any love that surrenders total agency to the interests of the beloved is sadomasochistic or mad, if you prefer that term. It has lost touch with the reality of its own interests. Now as for the madness that incubates within the family dynamic it is, of course, very prevalent as many of my colleagues show, most notably perhaps RD Laing. But this modern fad of talking about 'dysfunctional families' I find unhelpful. Not because so many families are not in some way dysfunctional – indeed perhaps all of them are that – but because the very use of the term implies there is a functional norm that we all know about and share. That is not true, not yet anyway. Families become dysfunctional partly because they are secretive and inward-looking in everyday practice.

"May I add something else about the notion of dysfunctionality as it relates to what is commonly perceived as normative behaviour? It is gendered. It is coded in masculine language. After the event a man can tell the conjugal partner he has physically assaulted, and this frequently happens, that he's very sorry indeed but he only hit her because he loves her so much and is terrified of losing her affection to another bloke. And the woman believes him, not because she is stupid, but because she has something very different emotionally invested in the marriage than he has, - different needs to do with the quality of love and the security of attachment. In part I concede ideology is at work here for the wife but it is not just that. A woman is biologically different to a man. She is a potential child-bearer and her instincts are geared towards that exclusively female direction of species destiny. Therefore she is dependent on her partner's love and support in a way he isn't on hers. Our anatomical sciences, so much of which are biologically reductive, fail to make this distinction. A woman thinks differently from a man because she feels differently from him, and she feels differently from him because her physiological purpose is different to his."

Suddenly the radio voice died and Johnnie's replaced it. "Come on in, Richard," he said. "I've finished the Fletchers' report and was just catching up on a radio programme while it prints out." Weller smiled as he entered the room, exuding avuncular affability. "Do you want a copy?" Johnnie asked.

"May as well take a gander," Weller beamed. "That woman being interviewed, Martelli, she's my ex mother in law, you know." Johnnie raised his eyebrows with surprise. "Did I never tell you?" Johnnie shook his head. "I mean in a manner of speaking. Penny, my wife, was brought up by foster parents. She never got on with them. And I never recognized the emotional damage they'd done to her until after we were married either. Penny couldn't stop flirting with other blokes. She was desperate for attention. When she was twenty she discovered her blood mother, Barbara, a rather aloof over-cerebral woman with a chip on her shoulder – as you've just been hearing. When we split up, Penny and me, and Penny tragically died I'd gone to live abroad and Barbara took charge of our two kids."

"I knew someone did, you told me, but I'd no idea it was her. That makes you almost famous," joked Johnnie to lighten the atmosphere. "When did you last see your children?"

Weller's ready smile darkened. He sighed and for a second almost became tearful. "I've never seen them since," he confessed. "I think of the past like Pandora's Box. It needs to be kept tightly locked." After a long silence he suddenly brightened and said, "Please don't stop listening on my account. The old girl's become as nutty as a fruitcake. I reckon she's got dementia. You find her entertaining, do you?" Johnnie contrived a half smile and shrug. He felt Weller's antennae probing deep into his motives. "The older we get the more cranky and superstitious, I suppose. Anyway, I'm off out again in a few minutes," Weller added. "Another chinwag with La Frayne. We're on the cusp of tying up a very lucrative deal and he needs to know you are still on board the flagship."

"Of course. Why shouldn't I be?" countered Johnnie. Weller nodded and turned away back through the door. "Good luck," Johnnie called after him. Almost simultaneously his mobile buzzed into life and he answered to the voice of Sarah.

"Sorry I didn't get back to you yesterday," she began. "I spent ages helping my sister to redraft an assignment and forgot." Johnnie expelled a sigh of relief. "How are you both?" he inquired. "Oh, we're fine. I received a letter from one of my dad's old friends today. He saw my ad in The Guardian. He's now a vicar in the Welsh borderlands and invited me to come and see him. I'm really thrilled."

Johnnie felt pleased for her. "I can hear it in your voice," he said and added hopefully, "Where are you right now? Anywhere south of the river? Can we meet?" Sarah apologized again. "I'm in Vauxhall waiting for a class to assemble," she explained. "Donna's just texted me. She's skived off college and gone to – "

"Piccadilly," interjected Johnnie. "How did you know?" demanded Sarah. "Er? The word just popped into my head," blustered Johnnie. "You are a one off. You should be on the stage with a talent like that!" said Sarah.

"What did you want to see me about anyway? It sounded urgent."

Johnnie could see the scene clearly now. It wasn't Piccadilly Circus but a bit down from there. A church and a courtyard set back from the main road, several trees like magnolias and a crowd of people. "I can't talk freely at the minute," Johnnie answered conspiratorially. "I'm at work. When can we get together?" Sarah hesitated before saying, "I'm very busy the next few days. I'll probably take Thursday and Friday off and shoot over to Wales. Can it wait til after I come back?"

"Of course," said Johnnie. "Sarah? I think she's in danger. Donna, I mean." Sarah emitted a spontaneous squawk of panic. "I'm sorry to lay it on you," he apologized and wanted immediately to bite his stupid impetuous tongue. "I just sense it. Not in danger today maybe. But I can't be more precise. Oh God, I shouldn't have said anything. I don't want to alarm you. It may be nothing at all."

St James Church, a short stroll from Piccadilly Circus towards The Royal Academy, was one of Donna's favourite London haunts. Artisans of all sorts were encouraged by a liberal Anglican vicar to ply their trade in the paved precinct and Donna always found a warm welcome whenever she established a pitch. Spring sunshine had produced droves of tourists. Two watercolour paintings of suburban landscapes had already been snapped up by couples from Boston and Tokyo respectively. She sat by the railings sketching a purple blossoming magnolia tree when her mobile sprang into life. "Are you alright?" demanded a breathless Sarah. "Yes. Why shouldn't I be?" responded Donna taken-aback. "Didn't you get my text message?"

Once Weller had cleared off Johnnie put the i-player back on. "Nutty as a fruitcake," he repeated to himself contemptuously. "The man's a bloody philistine."

"May I read you part of a review of your book written by Monsignor Geoffrey Franklyn?" asked the interviewer. "'This distinguished author whose subtle observations about the human condition I have much enjoyed in the past suddenly appears to be losing her academic marbles. It is one thing to deconstruct class and gender inequities, indeed to thoroughly question our all too complacent assumptions about the nature of sanity and the various pathological behaviours that pass for normality, but quite another to dabble in matters of the occult that classical science debunked decades ago. One concludes this book with the disconcerting impression that if Professor Martelli had her way we would be replacing penicillin with snake oil, open heart surgery with aura irrigation, IVF with pagan fertility rituals and prayer meetings with clairvoyant séances. The universe may well turn out to be far stranger than we presently imagine but surely what ordinary people need to protect them from the rigours of mortality is a solidly reliable religious faith and not the open ended anarchy of metaphysical speculation proposed here?' Your comments please, Professor Martelli."

It sounded to Johnnie as if Martelli was trying to stifle a chuckle. "Well, where to begin?" she said. "Let's try the occult. It's a term that means hidden or secret. Occultists are people who claim to have clandestine knowledge, relating to the laws and processes of reality. An occultist might therefore be able to walk on water, levitate, heal by touch etc. Jesus did all these occult things and more, if the gospels are accurate. And he preached repeatedly about the hidden world that existed beneath the visible material one. He implored his followers to seek it out constantly. In Mark 4 for instance Jesus says, 'Whatever is hidden is meant to be disclosed and whatever is concealed is meant to be brought out in the open.' In Mathew 13 he says, 'The kingdom of heaven is like treasure hidden in a field.' Jesus talks as if something beatific and transcendentally blissful is encoded in ordinary material reality. He calls it the kingdom of heaven and describes it in numerous elliptical parables.

"Now as a senior Catholic Monsignor Franklyn is required to believe that Jesus was the first person in the entire history of humanity to perform these occult miracles. Jesus is not an occultist, therefore. According to doctrine he must be the only begotten conduit of God. And if you firmly subscribe to that doctrine you too may be visited by the Holy Spirit and become endowed with a flavour of Jesus's supernormal power. By this logic any non-Christian who claims to be able to perform such miracles is either a stage magician or the spawn of the devil. So if I come along – and I'm by no means the only one – and reveal an abundance of evidence that demonstrates such supernormal activity can also be perpetrated by secularists and by those of an alternative religious persuasion, then I am in Franklyn's terms an apostate. This evidence I bring to bear in my book - which is why Franklyn is so furious with me. Franklyn is not opposed to occultism, he just wants occultism on his own exclusive narrow terms."

At some point Donna went to use the church toilet and when she came back a middle-aged white man was earnestly studying the drawings she had left on display. "You've certainly got a talent. Whose this?" he asked indicating a portrait of Sarah. She told him and the man nodded, carefully ruminated then said, "Would you be kind enough to draw me? I'd be happy to pay any reasonable fee." Donna would have done it for nothing. The man had an interesting face and an ultra polite manner. "Okay," she smiled obligingly and found him a wicker chair to sit on.

"The established Catholic church wants us quite rightly to create a more equal and forgiving and compassionate global society," Martelli was concluding, "but it does not want us to stand on the cutting edge of knowledge. Because when we do stand on the cutting edge of knowledge then the force of natural creation that Catholics call God turns out to be far more subtle, elusive and paradoxical than they ever imagined. Just think of the paradox of the infinitely expanding post-Big Bang universe – expanding into what exactly? Think of Schrodinger's cat, dark matter and black holes. The places to which quantum and cosmological science have taken us are beyond bewildering.

"As for snake-oil, by which I take it Franklyn means the placebo in general, it has been shown in carefully monitored scientific trials to have a significant success rate. Right now science has no idea how the placebo effect physiologically works but when we eventually find out and refine the technique, the resource implications for our financially over-stretched health service are enormous. Of course curiosity and the ethical practice of curiosity must have sensible limits imposed upon it. But how those limits are imposed and who imposes them is open to further careful debate. And I have serious doubts that the church of God on the one hand or the church of Scientific Materialism on the other are competent to conduct it."

A small crowd of onlookers stood admiring Donna's artistry, her impeccable concentration and eye for detail. When the portrait was finished and signed the commissioning customer studied it appreciatively too for a full minute before opening his wallet and pressing a wad of bank notes into Donna's hand. "Sixty pounds!" she gasped. "Nobody pays me that much." The man merely grinned and insisted it was worth much more but that was all he had on him.

"I'm on my way to the Van Gogh exhibition at The Royal Academy, Donna," he said. "I don't suppose you would care to join me? My treat." Donna thanked him and explained she had visited it three times already and that Vincent was her favourite painter. "I'm a trustee of Tate Modern," he told her, "and soon we are holding an exhibition of Anthony Orwell's work. Take this flyer and if you happen to be free that day it would be my privilege to show you round at the official opening. Just ask for me at reception when you come. I shall be there from 10am."

"Thank you so much. I might do that," replied Donna studying the leaflet. "But I don't even know your name. What is it?"

The man had already begun to turn away. "Just ask for Edgar," he said over his shoulder. "Edgar Laidlaw."

TRUTH AND FALSEHOOD

**11** Having framed then hung Donna's portrait in his lounge Laidlaw went to email one of the numerous art historians with whom he globally corresponded about the precocious artistic talent he had just discovered in a churchyard when something appalling occurred. A brazen message appeared from Luke Karamba demanding his attendance at a seminar. "Edgar! Listen up!" it screamed. "The secret of financial success is about to be yours!" The junk mail firewall had somehow been breeched and when three more Karamba promotions arrived in fairly rapid succession a crimson mist descended in Laidlaw's mind. *This is the bullying, unacceptable face of free market capitalism*, the mist informed him. *Such moral apostasy has to be repudiated in deed as well as word.*

Two days later when Sarah Atkinson set out to rendezvous with the Australian thesbian, Sinclair Scott, in a Kilburn High Road pub she had no inkling of the tremors of anxiety she had inadvertently incubated in his heart. It had not initially been a problem when his agent called to say Sarah Atkinson wanted to chat with him. Why not? he thought and gave the green light. But then a second call from a man he had not seen for fifteen years on the same subject seriously spooked him. "Hullo, Sinclair. This is Richard Weller," he had heard. The actor was inebriated, a state he increasingly indulged on non-working days and a long pause ensued on Scott's part before the penny finally dropped. "I bumped into a very unlikely splinter of our mutual past recently and I wanted to share my discomfort," Weller had confided. "Don Atkinson's daughter, Sarah. I played mutt, of course. But she's got hold of my company address and been emailing me all sorts of questions about her dad and his friends. I don't like it."

"Jesus, Weller, she's been on to my agent for a meet up!" replied Scott. "And I actually agreed to it! There's no way she could know anything, is there? Has she been on to Williamson, too?"

"I haven't seen Williamson since way back when," said Weller. "Perhaps he's had a religious conversion and his conscience has been pricking him? Or perhaps the hatchet Williamson hired has been spilling his guts to the police? What I suggest is you meet her and find out what exactly she's digging for then get back to me. Okay? It may be nothing."

The weather had taken a turn for the worse and Sarah arrived a bit sodden at the Kilburn pub. As she folded up her umbrella a wizened figure with longish grey hair gestured her over to a corner where he sat nursing a beer. He stood up as she approached and said, "Sarah! What do we do after all this time, embrace or shake hands?" Sarah offered him her cheek. She was surprised by his familiarity. "You mean we've met before?" she said. "I had no idea."

The face was wrinkled and weather tanned, the eyes a piercing blue, but nothing about the composition of the Australian's angular features or his husky voice raised so much as a ripple in her memory. "Why should you?" grinned Scott. "You were knee high to a penguin and I was a beanpole – still am in fact. Do you remember that pre-school nursery you were in? I went there a couple of times with your dad to collect you. The last time I saw you was at your sister's christening party."

It was while she was waiting at the bar to buy his fourth pint of Guinness that Sarah decided Scott was a devious unctuous toad. If she dropped a name from Don's journals Scott adopted one of two positions. Either he celebrated them as paragons of talent or he simply didn't remember them. Endless jolly anecdotes proliferated about Don, Reg and himself in their cohabiting years trying to crack the British theatrical establishment but all felt carefully sanitised to Sarah with everything ugly airbrushed out. Reason told her Scott was just being sentimentally nice to her, intuition that he calculated like a wheedling politician.

After a while Sarah had taken to studying his eyes, all tiny semi-glazed squints and blinks. These, not words, were the real tells that fed her insight. The most glaring tick came when she mentioned the TV producer, Martha Bassinger. "Yes, a truly delightful, intelligent woman. I knew her a bit and even dated her once or twice," he replied before sidetracking swiftly into, "Let me tell you about the house-warming party your mum threw in Greenwich where I first met Grace." Fina, the name mentioned more than any other in Don's notebooks, Scott did not recognise at all and this time Sarah believed him. "Let's do this again sometime and the tab will be on me. Okay?" said Scott as she beat her retreat.

"Okay," agreed Sarah with dilute gratitude. What she felt now as she walked out of the pub was disappointment more than anything else. Never mind, she still had Martha Bassinger to see later that same day. How glad she was not having made the mistake of mentioning it to Scott!

Outside the rain was still falling relentlessly and she realised that she had forgotten to pick up her umbrella. Sinclair Scott did not notice her re-enter the pub. He had repositioned himself at the table with his back to the bar and was furtively engrossed in a mobile phone conversation. As she picked up the brolly Sarah heard him say, "Yeah, she's just left this minute, Weller. I don't think we've got anything to worry about. It strikes me as just a grief thing. You see, her mum's kicked the bucket and the kid seems to be on this weird trip down memory lane.......... No, I don't think there's any need to speak to Williamson on the business matter but, on the other hand, it might not do any harm either, if you can track him down."

Later when Sarah hooked up with Martha in a Hampstead wine bar a very different story became evident. "You may find this hard to credit looking at me now, Sarah, overweight and over made-up to hide the wrinkles, but that Sinclair guy was obsessed with me," revealed Martha. "Possessive, jealous, insecure, suffocating - these are not toxic enough words to describe him. He was by far the worst misjudgement of my life. After a couple of months my flatmate left and I invited him to take her place. It was okay to begin with but he couldn't get any work and was dossing around while I had this full-on McCawber Square show to manage that had taken off big time with the public. You know how all sorts of rumours fly around a soap opera studio – or perhaps you don't? Most of it's just contrived by the producers to feed the tabloid publicity machine. Anyway Sinclair bought into it. He assumed

I must be screwing every actor who popped his head round the door wanting a part. And he could get violent. I had a few bruises to show for my trouble. When I tried to tell him we were incompatible and ask him politely to leave he roughed me up. Actually he moved between states of morbid self-pity, threatening to commit suicide, and violent hysterical tantrums. He was a well screwed-up, manipulative individual!

"This was where your dad came in. I met Don when he first got a job script writing for McCawber Square. We got on famously. Your dad was a very attractive man. He had this irreverent mischievous personality that seemed to endear him to men and women alike. He was quite tactile and he asked a lot of questions, too many actually for some people's liking. But when you got to know him you realised there was a serious, uncompromising side to his nature. He was constantly trying to devise ways to outrage or subvert conventions. Anyway, your dad eventually interceded and persuaded Sinclair to move out. He succeeded where everything else had failed. Don charmed him out. He sweet-talked his old mate into a studio flat and even paid the deposit on it for Sinclair.

On top of that as another inducement Don introduced him to Harry Merton who was looking for a gawky stooge for a TV sketch show he was making. Not that Sinclair ever properly appreciated the favours. He was an oily creep, Sarah. The acting world is a very small claustrophobic space and he didn't want to make an enemy of your dad, especially as Don's star was in the ascendant. You can imagine what Sinclair really assumed, can't you? That Don was making out with me! Sinclair came round one night drunk as a skunk and laid some pretty evil stuff on me, I can tell you. He said he was going to have Don sorted out. Don just laughed when I told him. He thought it was a huge funny. Apparently Sinclair had just been round to see him with a hundred quid he owed Don and a bottle of Scotch. They'd even sat down and drunk half of it and Sinclair had gushed that Don was the best bloke he'd ever known. 'But he wants to kill you!' I insisted to Don. 'Sinclair's eyes were all bloodshot with rage and he meant it!' Your dad cracked some joke about the way drunken Aussies talk to their mates. 'I'm going to have him sorted is the closest most of them can get to saying, 'I love you like a brother', Don laughed.

I couldn't believe it when I heard Don had been killed in a freak road accident. I was in Manchester then. I'd taken a job with Granada. It still makes me shudder just to think of it."

On the way back from Hampstead via Waterloo to St Margaret's Sarah remained too preoccupied with her own agitated thoughts to notice the late headlines blaring from newspapers and television monitors. Somebody had been killed in broad London daylight, shot dead in a public place and the killer had got away. And it was not until the train reached Putney when she heard a passenger seated opposite say callously to his friend, "Good bloody riddance - his bandits have been pestering me for weeks!" that she realised the victim in question was a certain American internet entrepreneur called Luke Karamba.

 Over a week had passed and the police had no leads on an apparently motiveless murder in a busy central London street. The pressure was growing, according to the news pundits. The Met were desperate for an arrest. And these were exactly Edgar Laidlaw's private sentiments as he obligingly showed several of their number around his home. They were on the upstairs landing now and one of them was staring at the ceiling. "That hatch gives access to the roof attic," Laidlaw explained. "I throw all my junk up there. Be my guest." A signal was given to one of the uniformed minions who secured the rickety wall ladder in place and trod gingerly upwards.

Laidlaw had previously been asked if he knew of Luke Karamba and had attended any of Karamba's wealth creation seminars. The officers had reassured him it was just one of numerous routine enquiries and he was not under suspicion. However Laidlaw had also been asked to disclose his whereabouts at the time of the murder, a detail that suggested otherwise. Clearly a reasonable balance had to be kept between polite cooperation and moral indignation, he reflected. Too much emphasis either way would not help his cause. "I can't really allow that!" complained Laidlaw when the senior officer asked if they could take his computer away. "I use it every day. And what help could it possibly be to you?"

The detective smiled benignly as if he had merely asked to borrow a cup of sugar. "We shall of course leave you with an alternative machine," he explained affably, "and allow you to download all your files on to it first. You see, sir, you did send an extremely vituperative, dare I say menacing email to Mr Karamba just two days before the murder, didn't you?"

Twenty women had packed into Sarah's living room, three of them newcomers. "It's lovely to see you and my gratitude to Sarah for hosting the event," Joc began and caught the eye of Joanne Cunningham who had introduced herself as a single mother who worked as a nightclub hostess. "We are just one of some thirty women's support groups colloquially known for networking purposes as The Unreasonable Club," Joc explained. "Let me get that name thing out of the way first. It derives from George Bernard Shaw who once wrote that reasonable people adapt themselves to the world while unreasonable people adapt the world to themselves – and concluded therefore that all progress depends on unreasonable people. Except back in those good old pre-emancipation days Shaw used the term men not people."

Mike and Donna were drinking in one of Brighton's Kemp Town pubs. "So how come you don't go to Sarah's women's group meetings?" Mike asked.

"Most of that sort of talk goes over my head," Donna giggled at Mike's seriousness. "In any case I had a far better offer on the table today – to visit you!" Mike nodded but had got no further than the first two words of his supplementary question when Donna cut in. "Sarah's got this theory about you," she confided. "You ask people a lot of questions not because you want to know the answers but to protect yourself from being asked questions yourself. Go on!" she continued in response to Mike's silence. "Tell me the really important stuff about you, the unvarnished truth. Show me your emotional vulnerability."

Mike took a long methodical gulp of beer. "Okay, I'll try," he said meekly. "When I was little I used to get frightened a lot, especially alone in bed at night. The infinity of blackness outside the window seemed to be swallowing me up, mocking my utter insignificance in the universe. There was no God in our house. We weren't a religious family, just the opposite in fact. My dad told me to jeer back at the void, to give the cosmos a two fingered salute. So that's what I did but the terror didn't go away, it just became shoved out of sight and camouflaged over with the usual boyhood distractions. I became very keen on outdoor pursuits. I'd push myself to the limits of whatever I was doing. One day, I must have been about ten, I went to the local woods to climb trees. It was a freezing cold winter morning. Snow lay several inches on the ground and nobody else was around. There was one particular tree that I'd never been able to climb more than half way up. Don't ask me what type it was, Donna. I only saw trees as physical challenges not plants!"

"Don't tell me you fell down?" gasped Donna with a sudden spasm of intuition. Mike nodded as if muted by memory. "Is that why you walk with a limp?" asked Donna clutching at Mike's hand.

Mike gathered himself together and explained that a branch had given way just as he reached the top. "I lay in the snow the rest of the day and all night until I was finally discovered in the morning," he said. "You see I never told my parents about my secret adventures for fear they'd forbid them. Anyway the whole experience was nothing like as bad as it sounds. In fact it was a revelation. It changed my life." He looked at Donna distrustfully now but saw her eyes overflowing with love and empathy. "While I was lying there virtually paralysed I felt this strange presence. It came right up close to me. I couldn't see anything though. I could barely move my head. But this presence, I call it that for want of a better word, made me somehow feel warm and comfortable. It began to talk to me. Talk is the wrong word. I couldn't hear words as such. It was the sense that somehow communicated itself to me. The sense was to not fall asleep, to rub snow in my face if I began to doze off. The sense reminded me of all kinds of personal things about myself nobody else knew, and it impressed on me the need to hang on because help was coming and I had a very important purpose to fulfil in my life. You know, Donna, after I was rescued I was in hospital for over a year and had several major operations but I never felt anything other than serene and happy in all that time. Yes I experienced pain but I didn't suffer. Does that make sense?"

At the end of the meeting when Sarah made a point of light-heartedly checking how many of the newcomers had been converted to the cause of "unreasonable" feminist action she discovered Joanne gazing at the mantelpiece family photograph taken at Donna's christening. Joanne confirmed the energy and camaraderie of the discussion had been enjoyable and said she would definitely come back. "But I don't think it's true all women who work in the sex industry are necessarily exploited," she added.

"I read an article by Pamela Stephenson arguing it was entirely possible for sex workers to be the architects of their own lives. In fact they provide an essential relief service for a certain type of bloke. I mean ones who are very shy and can't get a partner, or old or physically disabled, or got some other personality problem. I'm intrigued by this photo, Sarah." Joanne pointed with her index finger. "One of the group is a dead ringer for a bloke I used to know," she said. "A younger version anyway. Look."

"That's Martin Williamson," replied Sarah. "He was a friend of my mother, Margaret. Excuse me a second. Joc is calling me. Yes, Joc?" But the embryonic conversation was never completed because when Sarah turned back to Joanne it was only to find her guest had slipped inconspicuously out of the house.

Two days later in a stuffy Whitehall office a cabal of policemen were deciding what to do next about the Karamba killing. The case against Edgar Laidlaw was barely even circumstantial but they had no other suspect in the frame. A question had been asked in the Commons. Two affronted republican congressmen had issued statements of concern. "The frenzied shooting of a distinguished US businessman in front of a dozen witnesses obviously isn't the work of Al-Qaeda," one sniped. "So what exactly is the great British bobby doing?"

What the senior "bobby" designated to brief the deputy chief constable, no less, was "doing" included a summation of the evidence against Laidlaw, starting with his alibi. "First, the suspect claims to have been in a cinema," he said, "a fact confirmed by the ticket clerk who knew him. But the cinema was twenty minutes walk from the murder scene so it's possible the suspect could have slipped out of an exit unseen. Second, all the witnesses describe the killer as stocky to fat with red hair whereas the suspect is medium build and bald. Nobody was able to identify the suspect at a line-up. He could have been padded up and wearing a wig, of course. Third, forensics found nothing in the suspect's home or lock-up to link him to the crime. He does, however, have a conditional discharge for aggressive behaviour and the hard drive of his computer reveals an interest in guns.

The suspect's explanation that he went through a period of hyper-anxiety about being burgled sounds less than plausible." He looked at his team and asked, "Anything else?" Nobody spoke. "Any hunches then?"

"My hunch says he's a nutcase and guilty, sir," offered one officer. "But there's absolutely nothing to make it stick. And what makes it worse is he's an intelligent nutcase and plausible. He's too far up himself to know the difference between night and day. He believes his own lies." And these remarks were greeted with virtually unanimous murmurs of assent.

FEELING AND THOUGHT

13 The North London Women's Writing Cooperative held their meetings in a primary school assembly hall just off the Finchley Road. It was easy to find and the guest received a warm reception. Many of the members of the cooperative had read Martelli's biography of Mary Wollstonecraft, published in the late 80s, not to mention non-members like Jocelyn Merryweather who hurried in breathless just after the introductions had been completed.

"It is really heartening to see your group so abundantly flourishing," Martelli was saying. "The other day I stumbled upon that Auden poem, you know the one in which he declares that poetry makes nothing happen, it exists solely in the valley of its own saying? Well I suppose that may be true for a bookish masculine stiff upper lip don't frighten the horses sort of poetry but it does not have to be true of all poetry, indeed of all creative writing. Words powerfully articulated can make things happen. They are a prelude to action. I recall Margaret Mead saying to me once, 'Never doubt that a small group of thoughtful committed citizens can change the world. Indeed it is the only thing that ever has!' So when you say in your manifesto, 'Our aim is not just to describe the world but to transform it for the better,' I say 'Here, here! And more strength to your writing elbows!'

"What I really want to talk about tonight, with your permission, is the disjunction between feeling and thinking in our culture, the imbalance between reason and emotion. And by the way, if you want to stop me at any point and ask a question please feel free. I notice Mary Midgely in analysing this phenomenon from a philosophical point of view concludes that 'Fear of and contempt for feeling make up an irrational prejudice built into the structure of European rationalism.' And I believe with a few notable exceptions we can see the same fear and contempt running like a vein through the mainstream tradition of poetry and literature. We have the centenary of the outbreak of the World War One almost upon us and we know numerous commemorations and documentaries are being planned. That is how it should be. After all this was supposed to be the war that would end all wars, and something since has gone badly wrong. What is it? Yes, I'm asking. Anybody?"

Several hands shot up and Martelli invited one of their owners to speak. "Men still run the world," she declared. "And men are violent and aggressive and warfare is their aphrodisiac. They cannot settle differences in any other way."

Once the clapping and laughter had abated Martelli resumed with, "I'm not going to quibble with your answer but I simply encourage you to watch out for all those forthcoming tribute to the fallen programmes and note how infrequently, if ever, that obvious point is made. Now back in the mid 1930s when the second world war was cranking up one of the doyens of the poetry establishment, WB Yeats, was commissioned by the Oxford University Press to select an anthology of modern verse and he excluded a number of poets such as Wilfred Owen who had written brilliantly about trench warfare, giving the reason for doing so as follows: 'Passive suffering is not a theme for poetry. In all the great tragedies, tragedy is a joy to the man who dies; in Greece the tragic chorus danced.' For Yeats it wasn't just that Wilfred Owen's poetry was 'all blood, dirt and sucked sugar' as he wrote to someone after a few complaints about the exclusions arrived, it was that Owen's war poems had been published with a manifesto that stated, 'Above all I am not concerned with Poetry. My subject is war and the pity of war. The poetry is in the pity.' I submit that for Yeats pity and compassion were associated with womanly states of being and as such were unfit to be proclaimed so promiscuously aloud by any kind of man, let alone a battle-hardened soldier. It was bad taste tantamount to literary apostasy. At the very least if a man is to describe his feelings he must do so in a tempered and controlled way, with a high degree of cerebral detachment. Had not Wordsworth, their predecessor in the great Eng Lit canon, said, 'Poetry is emotion recollected in tranquillity'?

"Yeats was not a run of the mill poet. He had won the Nobel Prize for literature and is still widely acclaimed by academics in the field as the greatest Anglophone poet of the 20th century. When taken to task for his dismissal of Owen, - I suspect the complainants were mainly women, - Yeats peevishly responded in a private letter, 'I did not know I was excluding a revered sandwich-board man of the revolution.' That was back in 1936. Has the situation changed today? Not that much, I fear. The privileging of intellectualism over feeling as a way of being still holds sway in science as well as the arts, and to challenge it has revolutionary implications for the staunch defenders of patriarchal hegemony.

"We must, however, take care not to tar all male writers with the same brush. Robert Frost more recently stated, 'Poetry is when an emotion has found its thought and the thought has found words'. That strikes me as precisely the order of the process. Emotion – thought - words. And not just in the art of poetry. In the art of science and in the art of every other creative endeavour. Alright, the thought can bounce back towards the emotion, indeed there can be a double or treble rebound between the two, a kind of pinball machine analogy occurs to me, and each bounce acts to modify the way the emotion is understood by the intellect – but the emotion is always the trigger, the starting point. As Frost writes elsewhere, 'A poem begins as a lump in the throat, a sense of wrong, a homesickness, a lovesickness.'

"In his epic poem, *The Prophet,* Kahlil Gibran writes that the soul is a battleground upon which our reason and judgement wage war against our passion and appetite," continued Martelli after a sip of water. "And he goes on to say that the discord and rivalry must be transformed into oneness and melody. Both are indispensable elements of our humanity. Unless we honour both 'house guests' equally then we become depraved, or certainly in danger of becoming so. 'Rest in reason and move in passion', Gibran writes.

"But in western civilisation and particularly in the field of science analytical reason certainly has the upper hand and authority. This situation derives directly from the ideology of patriarchy. In simple terms Descartes announced the Enlightenment with the words 'I think therefore I am' and nothing much has philosophically changed since. Men are emotionally buttoned-up, science is invented by men, ergo reason is privileged to the detriment of feeling. And as a consequence the science of the human self has become significantly distorted.

"You see this distortion in the bio-deterministic models of life, the essentialist dogma that people are reducible to their anatomical component parts. In a recent book, for example, Richard Dawkins asserts that "human emotions depend for their existence on brains". This is a crude caricature. We don't yet really know the anatomical home address of our emotions although we have discovered they travel all over our bodies and bind to neuropeptide receptors on the outside of cells. Anyone who has watched the clouds disperse to reveal the highest peak of Everest and felt their heart palpitate with awe or who has listened to Bach's St Mathew Passion and felt the hairs bristle on the nape of their neck knows that the brain is not uniquely the seat of the emotions. Dawkins also asserts that the human body is merely 'an elaborate machine for passing on the genes that made it.' Others like Francis Crick contest that free will is an illusion and our sense of agency is entirely determined by the neurons firing off in particular compartments of the brain. Such science ignores decades of research in sociology and psychology. It robotises our species. Altruism becomes impossible. As too does any constructive challenge to selfish and destructive collective behaviour. In this brave new world of what Hilary and Steven Rose refer to as '*Genes R Us*' and '*Neurons R Us*' rationality, human intentionality becomes an illusion."

A hand went up and Martelli allowed the interruption. "You have been criticised by several reviewers as providing succour for the superstitions and irrationalities of religion because you write about the human soul," asked Joc. "How would you respond to that?"

"Well, just because science hasn't yet located a biological organ it can identify as the soul does not mean it may not eventually do so. Perhaps it is looking in the wrong places and using the wrong methodology? When I use the term 'soul' I tend to mean the inner authentic sense of self. Alright we can debate the exact nature and habitation of the self but we cannot, I think, dismiss the fact one's sense of self changes in relation to ideological, interpersonal and other life experiences. It finds ways to protect itself from uncomfortable truths, for instance, and to create a false mask or acting persona that deals with the difficult and potentially painful business of the social world. These two selves or souls can in certain circumstances become dissociated from each other, of course."

"Like Dr Jekyll and Mr Hyde, you mean?"

"Yes. Dr Jekyll was the very essence of what one might figuratively call a lost soul."

"But you also suggest in *Heaven And Earth* that this authentic self or soul always retains a connection to its Original source via a faculty you call 'intuition'. That sounds like a very religious concept. Do you believe in God?" persisted Joc.

"Not in any simplistic anthropomorphic sense," Martelli replied. "Einstein said he felt like a little child entering a huge library filled with numerous books in numerous different languages. The child knows someone must have written these books but has no idea how. Equally he dimly suspects an order in the arrangement of the books but doesn't know what it is. So like Einstein's inner child I similarly experience a universe organised to an astounding degree of complexity and obeying certain laws but I only dimly grasp what those laws might be."

Martelli took another drink of water before continuing. "So intuition is really a suspicion, an instinctive feeling, and we ignore it at our peril. Someone once said, 'Intuition knows what to do. The trick is to let your head shut up and allow intuition just to get on with it.' This is how scientific inquiry works, first the 'feeling' then the cognitive verification and knowing. The challenge for humanity is to synthesise not just emotion and reason but also intuition and intellect. Oppenheimer in *Science And Human Understanding* wrote about 'these two ways of thinking, the way of time and history, and the way of timelessness and eternity.' Both constitute 'man's efforts to comprehend the world' yet 'neither is comprehended in the other nor reducible to it.' Neither the emotional intuitive mode nor the analytical reasoning mode tells the whole story.

"An Italian Psychiatrist, Roberto Assagioli, in his book *Psychosynthesis* illustrates how essential yet difficult it is for scientists to marry intuition and intellect into a creative working relationship. This is mainly because intuition does 'not work from the part to the whole, as the analytical mind does, but apprehends a totality directly in its living existence' - in its *being* - and its being 'is produced chiefly by eliminating the various obstacles preventing its activity.' Intellectuals often become afraid when 'an intuition intrudes into their thought processes; they are diffident and treat it very gingerly; in most cases they repress it,' says Assagioli. Like Einstein before him Assagioli insists that, of the two, intuition provides 'the creative advance towards reality' whereas intellect translates into acceptable mental and verbal terms the results of intuition. 'A really fine and harmonious interplay between the two can work perfectly in a successive rhythm' he argues, 'intuitional insight, interpretation, further insight and its interpretation and so on'. Does that help?"

Joc nodded and smiled her appreciation. Several rows behind her a younger woman spoke up. "You say in the same book humanity has a vast reservoir of potential but exploits only a tiny amount of it. What do you mean by that exactly?" she asked.

"I suppose I mean at least two things," reflected Martelli. "The first has never been better put in my opinion than by Marianne Williamson in *Return To Love*, you know that much quoted passage used by Nelson Mandela when he left prison, 'Our deepest fear is not that we are inadequate. Our deepest fear is that we are powerful beyond measure. It is our light, not our darkness that most frightens us - '"

"We are all meant to shine, as children do?"

"Yes exactly. That one. Our 'playing small does not serve the world' yet so many settle for just that. Why? I think it is because the ideology of materialism has divorced us from our sense of origin and spiritual destiny. Our mortality, our ephemerality get continually rubbed into our faces. To be repetitive and mechanically reliable is as much as we need to offer to a world that has only old age and death to offer back to us. To be daring and energetically inventive is to risk ridicule and failure. I don't mean that to sound like a justification for the worst excesses of capitalism, by the way. William Blake wrote, 'Energy is eternal delight' and clearly he believed that human energy should be used for the elimination of poverty and social inequalities.

"The second thing I mean is to do with the way we approach the challenges of life. We approach them with a defeatist or false logic. Again it is about ideological indoctrination. Human actions, we are told, are always binary, that is right or wrong, successful or failed. You are a winner or a loser. You cannot be both. Well, why can't you? Wrong and failed are death knell words in our culture. They resonate dreadfully in the psyche and undermine it. But the truth is the overcoming of any particular challenge is a strategic process. You have to be wrong first to be eventually right. A battle may be lost but the war remains to be won. It's when you expect quick or easy resolutions that you often fall into despair and give up. Or when you are inflexible or obstinately over-earnest in the way you tackle the challenge. Be patient with a problem. Enjoy its complexity and beauty. Walk away from it periodically and when you come back view it from a different angle. The number of times I've gone to bed feeling totally blocked and woken up the next day with the resolution formed clear as crystal in my mind. That's how intuition works. It stays alive even when we are asleep. And it takes us into the most wonderful and unexpected directions. Without it we could not be creative. And in the excitement that's generated by this process we become connected to that entity I have called Origin. If that sounds religious I apologise. Sorry, on reflection I withdraw that apology. To feel ones-self a player in the creative processes of reality, however small a bit part player, isn't that the essence of what religious experience really is?"

FREEDOM AND CAPTIVITY

 "You'll be okay while I'm away, won't you?" Sarah asked her sister over breakfast. Sarah had booked a ticket on the 10.35am train from Paddington. There would be two changes en route to Leominister where her father's old friend Reg had kindly agreed to meet her on the station platform. "What are you going to do today?"

"Well, my classes finish at noon," replied Donna with a sarcastic roll of the eyeballs. "After that I think, with your permission, I might head for Tate Modern. There's a preview of a new Anthony Orwell exhibition on today. I'll give you a ring this evening. Okay?"

A bit later when they left home together to travel in different directions Sarah gave Donna a farewell hug and remarked, "There's a basket of ironing if you've got time. Have fun." It was the sort of radiant breezy spring day that permeates even the most arid soul with optimism. Arriving at Paddington thirty minutes early Sarah scribbled a brief note to Martin Williamson and posted it. "I have reason to believe you were involved in some nefarious scheme with Sinclair Scott and Richard Weller to the detriment of my father," it stated. "Within a couple of days I shall know the whole story. Much better therefore if you come clean to me now." It was a bluff, of course, a calculated shot across the psychoanalyst's bows that had been suggested by Jocelyn, but little did Sarah guess the spasm of remorse and anxiety it would precipitate in the recipient.

Remorse was not an emotion Edgar Laidlaw generally permitted himself. In his philosophy it represented the toxic puss of self-indulgence that oozed from putrefying memories. He had not been at all sure that Donna would turn up so his delight at renewing her acquaintance became expressed in multiple grand gestures of hospitality. He introduced her to other guests like Tracy Emin and Damien Hirst and gave her a tour of the concealed storage rooms containing works of art that, like the Gnostic scrolls secreted in the Vatican crypt, were considered too blasphemous to be placed before the public gaze. Laidlaw's aesthetic dexterity impressed Donna. Yet he always gave her opinions, however naively articulated, proper credence. "Where is Anthony Orwell?" she asked him as they took a detour into the general exhibition area to see some famous Damien Hirsts.

"Oh, he's not here in person. He's a recluse," said Laidlaw. "He never leaves Australia. What do you think of this?" Her host was indicating a glass fronted wall cabinet containing forty odd seashells in linear rows. It was called *Forms Without Life* and somebody, obviously not the artist, had written an interpretive blurb underneath for the hard of under-standing. After a couple of minutes inspection Donna opined, "I like the piece but I find the written interpretation a bit pretentious. The breathtaking beauty is in each individual shell not the way they've been assembled together. This is like the art of flower arranging to me. Nature is the real artist here, not Damien Hirst."

Laidlaw nodded and smiled. And so is most conceptual art, he thought to himself, secretly impressed by the intuitive intelligence of his guest as he escorted her to the next exhibit. "The best art is always a form of meditation and worship," he confided. "It puts you in direct relation with the eternal. Of course, the artist has to acquire a range of practical technical skills but having acquired them he has to use them unselfconsciously. He has to enter the experience he is trying to portray like an explorer entering uncharted territory, that is with complete trust in his navigational ability to get him to the heart of reality then safely back out again."

Donna liked this analogy. It was how she had come to think of Vincent Van Gogh. "Most conceptual art is the opposite of this," continued Laidlaw. "It is desperately attention seeking and undisciplined. It wants to shock and flabbergast the spectator. Conceptualism began as a legitimate rebellion against the values of the commercial art market in which a celebrity name could be used to camouflage and flog mediocre works at exorbitant prices; but like all rebellions it quickly degenerated into the orthodoxy and now stagnates in the increasingly vapid gravy of its clichés."

"Don was never short of an opinion, whatever the subject," Reg told Sarah on the drive from Leominster to Presteigne where the Australian had lived as the incumbent vicar for almost a decade. It was hardly news to Sarah. She had spent the journey from Paddington re-examining three of Don's most baffling journals. Two contained surreal jokes and stories, the third a rambling inquiry into the nature of linguistic codes and aesthetic composition. "I used to be an actor too, you may recall," said Reg, "but I rarely found work and when my agent dropped me I eventually returned to Australia and trained for the ministry. Presteigne," he chuckled, "is the kind of remote outpost to where British Anglicans dispatch their dissident priests and liberation theologians."

At the vicarage Sarah was convivially greeted by Reg's wife, Olwyn, and her two teenage sons from a previous marriage. "I've been nagging Reg to invite you since he spotted your advert in the Guardian," she said. "But like his God my husband moves in a wondrously slow and mysterious way!" The list of questions Sarah had prepared to ask Reg was so long she hardly knew where to start. Given Olwyn's sense of humour perhaps comedy might prove as good a place as any?

So after tea and Bara Brith cakes she produced one of Don's notebooks. "This is full of crazy jokes and stories. Let me give you a brief flavour. *A famous guru is delivering a discourse about Beauty. Everything in the natural world is beautiful, he insists, all you need to do is pay proper devotional attention to it and love it, switch off your conditioned judgemental mind. He goes on and on like this and finally this hideous old hunchback stands up and says, 'What about me? Am I beautiful?' The guru stares intently at the man for fully two minutes then replies, 'You are truly the most beautifully deformed hunchback I have ever seen.'"*

"And here's another," continued Sarah. "*One day a man was walking around the city muttering to himself, 'I hate them those vile profiteers, those liars and manipulators, callous greedy hypocrites. I hate them!' when a policeman approached and said, 'You are under arrest for insulting the government.' The man complained, 'I never mentioned the government once!' 'I'll admit that retorted,' the copper handcuffing the man, 'but you described them so perfectly.'* What sort of jokes are these, Reg? And why did dad become a comedian?"

Reg wiped a few tears of laughter, perhaps nostalgia, out of his eyes. "I think those jokes were borrowed from Bhagwan. Don studied with the bloke in India before he finally settled here," he replied. "Bhagwan's ideas influenced him a lot. Stand-up allowed him to reach a new public and explore the politics of subversion. There's nothing more subversive than laughter, he used to say. And Don believed we are all enslaved by the various ideologies peddled to us. Our very thoughts are tightly scrutinised and policed. But he also suspected the innate world, the world that is not conditioned by our psycho-social experience, to be perfect in form and that all creatures have an aesthetic sense that can recognise that structure."

"Was he spiritually inclined then my dad?" asked Sarah.

"He certainly read a lot on the subject," considered Reg. "Evelyn Underhill, William James, and he was into Lyall Watson and Colin

Wilson, too – anybody in fact who was trying to peel back the veil of ideology, as Don liked to call it, to get at whatever permanent truth exists beneath. Do you know any of those authors, Sarah?"

Sarah shook her head. "A couple by name only," she replied. "What did dad think about you retraining as a priest in a mainstream church?"

Reg laughed. "He never criticised or discouraged the idea," considered Reg. "Maybe he was too polite to tell me directly? I remember him once saying with a twinkle in his eye that genuine religion was too good for the religious. By which I take it he meant that faith should proceed from deep experience of numinous reality and not just be an unthinking Sunday morning parroting of credos. Oh yes, 'make sure you teach your flocks about the real Jesus', was another of his teases. 'The one who chucked the moneylenders out of the temple and allowed the whore Mary Magdalen to massage his body with expensive oils'."

"And do you?" smiled Sarah mischievously.

"Not quite in those precise terms," chuckled Reg and then reflected seriously for a few moments. "Don was politically apolitical, if that makes sense. He didn't need to burrow into the security of hermetically sealed orthodoxies like so many of us do. He thought human behaviour was basically irrational and every member of every tribe would get on a lot better with each other if they stopped pretending otherwise. 'It's almost impossible to find anyone who means what they say or says what they mean – at least for longer than half a minute a week,' he once quipped. And the proper use of language was incredibly important to him. 'Words properly constructed and delivered have magical properties', I remember him saying. Come on, let's go for a stroll round the parish!"

About six o'clock Donna felt so leg weary she needed to sit down.

"My wife was very impressed by your sketch of me," Laidlaw told her over a beverage. "In fact she would love to meet you but I suppose you are otherwise engaged tonight?" When Donna shook her head Laidlaw assured her they lived but a short cab ride away. "Wait a minute though," he suddenly hesitated, producing a phone from his pocket. "I need to check with Christabelle in case she's busy.....Hullo, Christabelle?......Yes. I'm still at Tate Britain. You know that portrait I've hung up in the living room? Well, I've bumped into Donna, the talented young artist who drew it, and I'm about to invite her round for a spot of supper. I think we may be able to persuade her to do more sketches.........Great idea, Christabelle! I'll ask her. See you later." He closed the mobile and turned back to Donna. "My wife was wondering if you might do her portrait after supper? Of course you'll be well paid."

Outside Laidlaw hailed a taxi. It negotiated Waterloo Bridge and The Aldwych through ever thickening traffic then, beyond St Paul's, Donna's sense of location became swallowed up in the amorphous mystery of north London. The journey passed quickly enough, however, as her companion plied her with friendly questions. When they alighted Donna noticed a 243 bus advertising its destination as Wood Green. "Where's Wood Green?" she asked as Laidlaw ushered her through the rickety iron gate of the terrace numbered 40. Seeming not to hear the question over the din of rush hour traffic, he produced a bunch of keys and began to unlock the front door.

"Christabelle, I'm home!" called Laidlaw as they passed inside. "Christabelle?" An odour of stale food hung in the air. "She must have popped out to the shops," suggested Laidlaw leading the way to the lounge. "Make yourself at home." The room had an old fashioned feel about it, - polished wooden floors, wrought iron fireplace, lace curtains and antique upholstered furniture. "Would you like a drink?" he asked. "I have some excellent cider." While he went to fetch it Donna's gaze moved swiftly around the walls. Besides the miniatures and photographs they contained, in a central position hung her very own portrait of Edgar, framed in ornate gilt, and her heart swelled with pride.

The truths Sarah learnt that night in Wales and on the following day about her father, indeed about her mother too, altered not so much the direction of her life but its texture. In *Heaven and Earth* Barbara Martelli comments in a passage not yet reached by Sarah, "Whatever stable sense of adult identity we secure is largely dependent on our parents because they are our first and most influential role models. Their silences, their absences and neuroses, come to define us every bit as much as their love and their counsel. We create meanings out of our parents' lives and we internalise those meanings so that unconsciously they evolve into the dominant landscape of our selfhood."

By 10pm Sarah suddenly found herself wondering why her sister had not been in touch. Instantly she got on the phone only to hit mechanical call-minders on both landline and mobile numbers. "Perhaps she's gone to bed?" yawned Reg. "It has been a long day." And like any good houseguest Sarah took the hint and turned in, too.

The next morning Donna opened her eyes on a strange shadowy landscape. A smell of marsh-land and the squawks of mechanical birds assaulted her fuzzy sensibility. Gradually the contours of a wall and a sink shaped out of the gloom. Her throat felt parched. She lifted her head now and realised she was lying in a narrow bed like a coffin. It had a roof just above her head held up by stanchions. It was a twin bunk like the one she had as a child. Suddenly, as if a sluice gate had opened in her soporific mind, the events of the previous evening came flooding through her consciousness. Edgar had cooked a meal. His wife had not arrived home, detained by some emergency, he said. He had played classical music while she had been making sketches and sipping cider. "I'll pay for you to take a taxi home," she recalled him saying but after that nothing. How had she finished up in a fusty subterranean dungeon? And where was her handbag? She padded across cold flagstones and yanked at an immoveable door-handle. "Is anybody there?" she called in panic. "I can't get out!"

 Barbara Martelli received a fair amount of mail, not all of it appreciative. It went with the territory of intellectual celebrity. Too self-effacing to take flattery seriously she rarely answered correspondents unless an unusually special reason compelled her. Johnnie Woo's letter fell into that category. "*Heaven and Earth* has provided me with hope that I am not insane or psychotic because I experience amazing coloured auras around people," he wrote, "and hear their minds thinking and intuit their life history and sometimes even their destinies. You use the phrase 'esoteric gifts' since science is not remotely close to explaining these bewildering human phenomena.

"I am 35 and thoroughly ashamed of my life, the majority of it spent working for a pimp trafficking vulnerable women from Asia to resource western brothels. What you call 'esoteric gifts,' for all it ever concerned me, were merely the provenance of cabaret tricksters. Then 3 years ago I underwent major surgery for testicular cancer and as I recuperated things began to change. The scales seemed to drop off not just my eyes but also my other senses. My awareness intensified a hundredfold. I became able to penetrate to the core of reality with absolute crystalline lucidity. It rendered me simultaneously awestruck and terrified and lonely. Who could possibly understand?

"I am appealing to you for help because I know you do understand. I know you can counsel me on how to break free from the criminal life that contains me, how to create a purposeful existence out of the debris of the old debased one. I once attended an LSE seminar of yours. If I have read your aura and your book correctly, Professor Martelli, you possess a generosity of spirit that will not deny me access."

Generosity of spirit was the precise phrase Reg had used to describe Sarah's father, Don. She reflected on it now, sitting in the sun-soaked vicarage garden while the vicar attended to various Friday morning pastoral commitments. Reg had slotted significant pieces into the Atkinson jigsaw puzzle although others still remained missing. "I met Don in 79 through an Earl's Court networking club and we decided to rent a shared house in East Twickenham," Reg had explained. "Sinclair Scott moved in soon after. Don's travelling had taken him all over the world. He talked quite a lot, as all we Aussies did, about our backpacking journey to the heart of European civilisation – Don's joke not mine - yet in many respects he remained a very private person, inscrutably so at times. He rarely mentioned his family in Melbourne. His father I inferred was a macho bully and his mother a shrinking violet. Occasionally Don talked about his older brother, Barry, and his close school-friend, Hilary. I think his family history embarrassed him."

At this point Sarah had mentioned her father's story about Ilario and Reg had surmised it might well have been based on autobiographical experience.

"Early on Don fell for a girl called Penny. She was a trainee teacher and worked part time as a barmaid in our local pub. I remember Penny was trying to reconnect with her blood parents. Apparently she had been adopted as a baby. She was devastated when Don split with her – about 3 years down the line. She took up with a city slicker bloke called Weller who drank in the same St Margaret's pub. Personally I didn't have much time for the bloke, too much swagger. I think Don tolerated him much better, maybe out of loyalty to Penny? I don't know exactly. I must have been back in Australia for at least a year when I heard they'd split up.

"In those early years acting jobs were hard to come by and Don started selling his writing and doing bits of teaching. I'm sure you know how he met your mother? She was a drama student at Goldsmiths and attended his acting work-shops. I tell you he was besotted. They got married just after she graduated. I was best man and Grace Ashton, Margaret's closest friend from Durham, the best woman, so to speak. Of course by then Don, Sinclair and I had long made separate living arrangements. We kept in touch but our careers diverged in different direc-tions. Don had a couple of plays produced on the London fringe then started getting script offers from TV. The stand-up comedy boom claimed him next. It was an enterprising time, new clubs opening every week.

"Alright, yes, he did play around with other women, I'm sorry to have to tell you. The affair he had with Grace almost had terminal consequences for the marriage. To be fair Don was consumed with remorse afterwards but Margaret went through hell on that one. We all envied the way women were attracted to him, especially tubby, follicly challenged men like me! But I can also tell you Don's love for your mum remained genuine and undiluted. He may have physically strayed but never psychologically, if that makes sense? I was back in Oz when the news of his accident came through. I think of it as my own personal James Dean moment. He was a shooting star alright but beneath the creative dynamism I always sensed a tragic vulnerability."

The ring tone of a mobile snapped Sarah out of her garden reverie and she hastened to answer. It was Mike Smith who had been trying unsuccessfully to reach Donna by phone. He sounded anxious. "Me too," replied Sarah. "If she's not at home all I can think is that exhibition preview spilled over into a party and she ended up kipping at someone's home." She made Mike promise to go to Tate Modern and ask some questions. It transpired Donna had arranged two days earlier to meet him at noon outside the BFI on the south bank and that was already thirty minutes ago! "How did Donna get access to the preview?" asked Sarah. "Those things are usually by private invite only, aren't they?" But Mike had no idea. "Please talk to their admin staff, they must have guest lists, and then ring me back," Sarah asked him.

Martin Williamson had just returned to his tenth floor consultancy room after a meeting with his fellow partners and was admiring the sleek unorthodoxy of the Gherkin building from the window when a call came through. "It's a Mr Richard Weller for you," said Silvia. "Do you wish to take it?"

"I wont be offended if you dispense with the pleasantries," he told Weller tersely. "What's up?"

"Sarah Atkinson. Have you been speaking to her about things you shouldn't have been?" came the retort.

"Certainly not. Have you? Or Scott?" snapped Williamson. Weller told him about Sarah's meeting with the Australian. "Not a clever thing to do. That bloke was fifty percent sugar two decades ago and the girl isn't stupid." He glanced at Sarah's letter, open on his desk. "But she's playing us. Take my word. By the way, I saw you the other day, Weller, going into a club in Belgravia I occasionally frequent. You blanked me."

"Did I? How rude. Must have had a lot of stuff on my mind," said Weller. "Are you receiving satisfactory service in there, mate?"

"Very much so – thanks for asking. But I never realised it was your business acumen providing it." Williamson heard a grunt. "Am I correct?" he asked. Then the line went dead.

"What's the matter?" asked Johnnie as his boss walked back into the inner office. "Bad news?" Weller instantly recomposed his features as if flicking a switch in his personality. Then Johnnie's own mobile vibrated into life. "May I?" he asked and received a gesture of approval. "This is Barbara Martelli," Johnnie heard. "Is it convenient to talk?" Johnnie could hardly credit his ears. "Er, not really," he replied desperately trying to escape from Weller's brazen stare. "The heat is on at work. Can I ring you back later?" Martelli obliged with a number that was hastily copied down and pocketed.

"Who was that?" asked Weller suspiciously.

"Just a friend," Johnnie lied. "I've told him before never to ring during business hours. Sorry."

"No need to be," smirked Weller. "You aren't actually busy." And he thought to himself, 'Just a friend? You're an inveterate loner, Johnnie. You haven't got any friends. Apart from me, that is.'

Over a late lunch Reg chatted about that savage contradictory decade of the 80's when virtually all forms of social radicalism were being strangled to death by Thatcherism and the spirit of progress had to take cover in whatever temporary bolt holes were available. "I took refuge in church ministry," he smiled, "and your father in satirical comedy. 'However dark the night becomes,' Don used to say, 'people of authentic truth and conscience have to find ways of keeping the flame of progress and freedom burning.' I don't think many really understood Don's passionate seriousness. He was too comedic and non-pompous in the ways he played it out."

When Sarah mentioned the allegations Martha had made about Sinclair Scott and her sense of a conspiracy against Don, also involving Williamson and Weller, Reg looked totally bemused. Nothing of the sort had registered with him and in any case Reg had only met Williamson casually once at a Christmas party the Atkinson's hosted. Similarly the name Fina had meant absolutely nothing to him. I never heard the word. "It could be code for something, an acronym? Don loved code words," was the best Reg could do.

Later on the train back to London Sarah had much to ponder. She felt disappointed in some respects but very gratified in others. There was still something essential lacking in the composite picture of her father. What was it? The stories she revisited in the journals now did make better, more complex sense, however. Fables or parables would be a better descriptor for them. Their sense operated at more than one level. Any fool could find in the text merely what his established preconceptions wanted to find. A person of 'authentic truth and conscience', however, would eventually disinter a deeper concealed meaning, carefully disguised by the code of language narrative.

But where did Don stand on gender politics? Sarah pondered. Had he condoned the same promiscuous free love behaviour in his wife that he condoned in himself? Just one notebook story pointed towards the possibility that Don endorsed the feminist discourse. "A very pregnant woman having disembarked at Heathrow after a flight from Columbia was questioned by an immigration chief," it went. "'What is inside that rotund anatomical swelling?' he asked suspiciously. 'Obviously my baby,' replied the woman contemptuously. Now Columbia is the cocaine capital of the world and many ingenious ways are devised to smuggle dope in. So a strip search was arranged and a false latex dome discovered attached to the passenger's body. 'Do you wish to change your story before we look inside?' demanded the chief angrily. 'Of course not!' replied the woman. Inside the dome the chief was amazed to find a beautifully moulded baby doll, utterly lifelike. 'So why do you carry this around?' he spluttered. The woman replied, 'Just to remind myself that giving birth is the most important task that anyone can ever perform and that the majority of men take the mothering process totally for granted.'"

South of Birmingham a call from Mike came through. He had drawn a blank. Nobody at Tate Modern knew who had invited Donna or recognised her from a photograph. Mike was clearly upset. Donna's phone still remained unattainable when he rang it. Maybe she's lost the thing? Sarah considered. There had to be a simple explanation. Then twenty minutes later her mobile burped again into life and the screen unfurled a text message. Her mouth fell open with trepidation as she read it: **chilling out nearby can u please allow us all time away i really need my own pad 4 a bit hope our bust up row not 2 b rptd 4+ nights then home i promise xxxxx donna ps feed boomerang**

 Sarah was struggling to contain her frustration. She had been in Chiswick police station ninety minutes now. They had taken a statement, confiscated her blackberry and lodged her to wait in a squat interview room that stank of urine. "I'm here to report the kidnapping of my sister," she proclaimed when the officers returned. "This is urgent. Why are you treating me like a criminal?"

The text message had been transferred to a sheet of paper and Sarah was asked to explain the code again. "Six x's means *read only every sixth letter*, Boomerang means *emergency*. Therefore the message is *in cellar no 40 br 24thr*," she repeated to sceptical frowns. "This kind of coding is not a perfect science," she continued. "There are ambiguities and abbreviations. I take *br* to mean 'bus route' and *thr* to mean 'three'. So what else can Donna be saying than she's imprisoned in a cellar at a house number 40 somewhere on the 243 bus route? And I've already checked! There is a 243 bus that runs from Tottenham to Waterloo Station! It should be a simple job for your people to check all the properties numbered 40 on the route."

Several miles away in Belgravia Joanne Cunningham, the latest recruit to Sarah's Unreasonable Club, nervously waited to see the voluptuous madam who managed the exclusive club in which she worked. A single mother of two with no educational qualifications and few assets, the servicing of affluent men had kept the wolf from Joanne's door for several years. She could not risk offending Madam Lucinda by declining an assignation, yet what this client called Martin had begun recently to demand of her favours felt like one sordid bridge too far.

Their little chat went badly. "Nobody else can do it, dear," Lucinda gently insisted. "With that blonde wig, your slender figure and eye colouring you are an absolute ringer for the poor dead woman Martin obsessively fantasises about. I've seen the photos he treasures of her. Of course I can understand how uncomfortable you feel about such role-playing but he's paying top dollar and your own rate has been doubled. I've known this gentleman for years. He's old school perv, clean and meticulously courteous. Pop along to the green room for make-up. He'll be here soon and I've got an executive meeting."

"The bastards didn't believe me," cursed Sarah. She was updating Mike who had driven over to rendezvous in a Chiswick pub. "It's too late now but tomorrow we're going to have to head over there early and check the whole bus route ourselves. Are you game?" Mike nodded. He had been listening in stunned silence. "And allowing her to send a text message?" mused Sarah hopefully. "That's the odd part. It suggests to me that whoever's got Donna may have a conscience of sorts. He's not just some random degenerate."

"He? It could be a she," suggested Mike. "Or a couple. Jesus God! I just remembered those two in Gloucestershire. What were they called? Fred and Rosemary West? The wife was totally dominated by the husband and they used to pick up innocent young girls from bus stops and he'd have his evil way with them before – "

Mike's larynx froze and Sarah's complexion turned spectral white.

At Chiswick police station DC Pauline White was reflecting on her superior's peremptory decision to write Sarah off as an attention-seeking hysteric with an over-active imagination and a criminal record. "But, sir, writing graffiti on a lap dancing club door and desecrating top shelf pornography magazines in a newsagent's are a different order of offence," Pauline told him privately now. "They may be construed as political protest actions."

"My view is that the sisters have fallen out, and the younger one is punishing the older by doing a disappearing act," considered the senior officer. "Look, keep an eye open and if this Donna hasn't come back home in a couple of days let me know. Okay?"

His two hours of lubricious, nostalgic bliss expired Martin Williamson pressed the exit button, blew a farewell kiss to "Margaret" and left the boudoir. Within seconds Lucinda had emerged from an adjacent room to conduct him discreetly out. The concupiscence was so immaculately stage-managed that he easily forgot such myth-making was a huge industrial business. "Was everything to your satisfaction?" Lucinda simpered.

"Absolutely delightful," he smiled. "I'd like to see Margaret again, say next Friday? There would be some slight modifications in procedure. I shall ring you up and explain." As Williamson walked down the steps to the pavement a taxi pulled up opposite and its passenger emerged. "Taxi!" he shouted, hoping to catch the driver's attention, then suddenly seemed to recognise the man leaving the vehicle. The stranger once again failed to reciprocate Williamson's interrogative stare as they passed almost close enough to touch shoulders. "Wandsworth," Williamson instructed the driver while never taking his eyes off the other man. Older, thicker in the girth but definitely Richard Weller, Williamson decided, as Lucinda opened the front door and Weller stepped quickly inside.

Come Sunday after a leisurely drive round the North Circular Sarah's makeshift plan went into action. A shining red Volvo Routemaster with its bold logo 243 WATERLOO stood idling in front of them. It was a quarter hour service even on Sundays. "Are you clear?" asked Sarah. "No unilateral action. We approach any suspicious property cautiously and together. Mike, my first alighting stop is Bruce Grove Station."

Sarah would ride the 243 bus, her job to reconnoitre and gain an overview of the territory, and Mike would follow after it in the car. They would remain in mobile contact with each other. Every sixth stop she would alight and compare notes with Mike. Then they would backtrack and investigate any properties with the number forty on the front door. Between Wood Green and the terminus at Waterloo there were sixty stops, a fact Sarah had ascertained from the bus company website. She knew the names of all the stops, too, but was less sure of the precise route the bus took from one to the other. That kind of detail had not been included on the company itineraries.

Johnnie Woo felt nervous. To be called to the boss's Richmond Hill penthouse was virtually unprecedented. "I had a final meeting in Belgravia last night with Christopher La Frayne," confided Weller stirring sugar into his coffee. "You know about the networks he controls?" Woo did not react. "We agreed a deal. A minimum of six girls each month up to an annual max of two hundred. It's cash on delivery. I need you to select and organise the transportation of the merchandise from the Far East. You leave Wednesday."

Woo took a deep breath and gazed out of the window across Petersham Meadows. "I'm sorry, Richard," he said. "I've made up my mind. I've got another job." It was nothing Weller subsequently asked that frightened Johnnie, the man retained an impervious mask as if listening with paternal concern. It was the way his aura changed from green and yellow to orange, magenta and finally to bright murderous scarlet. "I'm not at liberty to disclose the name of my new employer or her company," Johnnie insisted with all the composure he could muster. "You may rest assured, however, that all your secrets will remain safe with me."

Mike's mouth felt parched and he wanted to urinate. "Stop gaping and stand behind this tree with me," Sarah ordered him and he obediently shuffled into the clandestine position. They had been searching the bus route for over two hours and just found an excellent match, a terraced house numbered 40 and set back a bit from the road with a basement. "What do we do now? Call the police?" asked Mike apprehensively.

"We can't just do that without something more solid," replied Sarah. "We'll ring the doorbell." Mike emitted an involuntary shriek of terror. "I'll do the talking. You take up a position to the right of the door where the basement window is and try as inconspicuously as you can to see if Donna's down there."

"Inconspicuously? How do you propose I do that?" stammered Mike.

"Pretend your shoelace is undone or something. I don't know," snapped Sarah impatiently. "Head up now. Be confident." She led the way through an iron gate the few yards to the door and rang the bell in two prolonged bursts. Nothing happened. She rang it again and this time a rattle of chain and latch advertised the imminent presence of the householder.

Mike bent down as instructed and closed his eyes until the clunk creak of timber gave way to Sarah's voice saying, "I'm so sorry to bother you." When he opened them and peered upwards a middle-aged woman wearing a pink floral housecoat and curlers stood above his head beaming with pleasure. "You must be from the council," she gushed. "How good of you to respond so promptly and to come out on a Sunday! The rubbish bags are piled in the basement. Two weeks in a row your bin men have missed me. If I forget just one monthly payment of my council tax I get a stern legal warning! Such outrageous double standards! What's he doing down there?"

Mike returned a winsome smile and apologised. "My lace has come undone," he explained.

Barbara Martelli was busy at home preparing the text of a talk called *Science, Religion and Improbable Probabilities* she was scheduled to deliver on Wednesday evening to an assembly of Quakers, Unitarians and other assorted non orthodox church goers when the urgent ringing of the phone scuttled her concentration. "I'm sorry to disturb you," said Johnnie Woo. "I've just got out of the meeting with Weller.

He took my resignation very badly. No direct verbal violence but – "

"Look, Johnnie, I think you need to abandon that studio flat you're renting in Notting Hill as soon as possible and move in here," Martelli broke in. "I know what this man is capable of when you cross him." After they had finished speaking she considered all her other options. Clearly Weller and La Frayne needed to be brought to book for trafficking prostitutes but what would happen to Johnnie if she simply told his utterly unwholesome story to the police? This wasn't America and plea-bargaining did not operate in the same way. There had to be an alternative strategy. Now who do I know in The Met? she pondered.

As Sarah disembarked from her fourteenth 243 bus of the day at Melpham Street in the shadow of Waterloo's ornate concrete facade just after 4pm she knew the task had defeated them. They were both emotionally drained and hungry, having survived on a diet of crisps and tea since leaving home. In the end they had found eight properties numbered 40 on the bus route but none bar one with an obvious basement room or cellar. Three had been within blocks of flats, one a restaurant and another a bank. They had rung on doorbells and whenever they could not get a direct answer from a householder they had made enquiries with neighbours. Nothing even remotely odd or potentially suspicious had come to light. Something appeared to be wrong, either with their detective methods or the coded information Donna had sent.

"Let's go back to the police – a different station perhaps?" encouraged Mike. "Let's be assertive and insist they take action - or else!"

Sarah felt distraught. "Or else what?" she managed to retort sarcastically. "We complain to the legal ombudsman?"

SCIENCE AND RELIGION

 Johnnie was travelling in a taxi with Barbara Martelli to her next lecture venue. "I'd like you to sit at the front of the hall and concentrate on the audience," she told him. "You don't have to listen to me so much as listen to them listening to me, if that makes sense. Think of it as an exercise in disciplined empathy. If you find yourself flowing into the consciousness of any single individual don't inhibit the connection. Rather go along with the flow."

"And what if I don't feel any flow or make any connection?" asked Johnnie.

"Then you don't," shrugged Martelli. "This isn't a test. There are no right or wrong outcomes. Consider it as an experiment with truth, your own truth." She chuckled as she added, "It isn't just the prerogative of the men in white lab coats to experiment with truth, you know. We should all be doing it and on a regular basis."

"You don't think of yourself as a woman in a white lab coat then?" smiled Johnnie. "As a guru in the dark arts?"

This brought another chortle of amusement to Martelli's mouth. For a while they sat in silence, enjoying the insulated ride through late rush hour traffic. Eventually Martelli said, "The problem is the gross ego. It has to be recognised for what it is and dismantled. The ego exists, of course, on a collective as well as individual level. It exists in both science and religion which are not, as their conservative practitioners believe, independent ways of knowing. Science and religion are different sides of the same coin. It is the professionally inflated ego that keeps the distinction alive nowadays. At their worst both science and religion are agencies of social control. At their best they become the conduits of enlightenment, hope, progress and joy. Next left please, driver!"

"The thing about you is you sound so certain about the uncertainties of life," said Johnnie as the cab pulled to a halt outside a drab looking building in Bermondsey. "Me, I haven't felt certain about anything since the doctors surgically removed my testicles in a cancer hospital."

After they alighted and she had paid the driver Martelli turned to Johnnie and said, "I've come across it many times before. Serious injuries and medical impairments can transform people in the most radically unusual ways." She stopped speaking, aware suddenly of a male gaze drilling into their intimacy. But the instant she returned the stare the eves-dropper glanced away and lit a cigarette. "It's as if in nature when you deprive one faculty of expression another seems to develop to compensate for the loss," she continued more confidentially. "That's what appears to be happening to you – very probably. It's an aspect of adaptation and evolution nobody yet understands. Come on." Martelli led the way up a flight of worn stone steps and as she reached the portal Johnnie received the distinct visual impression of intense white light flooding out of her slender body.

It was a fairly undistinguished church hall with a vase of flowers alleviating the austere ambience but the turnout was better than she had expected. However a rather muted atmosphere of solemnity prevailed. "Good evening," Martelli eventually began. "I wonder how many of you are versed in probability theory?" There was virtually no reaction. "So I propose to begin with a short interactive survey," she continued and found no objection as she gazed around the predominantly older generation of a hundred and twenty attendees. "Please raise your hand if you believe there is a God." The response was nothing like unanimous. About two thirds of the audience reached for the ceiling. "Thank you," she said. "Now how many believe that Jesus of Nazareth was the only begotten son of God?" This time only three arms were raised of which two belonged to small children. Martelli gave the youngsters a smile of appreciation then said, "Now for the biggie. How many of you believe England will win the forthcoming world cup soccer tournament?" And not one person moved. Almost simultaneously a burst of incredulous laughter swept the hall and the ice was broken.

"Some of you may have heard of Thomas Bayes. He was a philosopher and mathematician who lived over two hundred years ago and probability theory owes him a great debt.

He devised the equation by which statisticians of all kinds still measure the probability of any particular event occurring today. I won't pretend I can teach you the complex algebraic formula of Bayes theorem. But I will tell you that a Manchester born physicist called Stephen Unwin came along much more recently and used the theorem to try to establish how probable it was that God existed. Applying Bayes theorem to six evidentiary areas – moral evil, natural evil, goodness, intra-natural miracles, extra-natural miracles and sentient religious and spiritual experiences - Unwin's mathematical conclusion was a 67% probability that God existed. Strangely that's about how many of you put your hand up.

"Now you are a sophisticated liberal congregation so as soon as I asked you to indicate whether you believed in God I'm sure the question arose, 'Well, it depends what you mean by God.' So here is another question that might induce a similar response. Would you mind if my friend, Johnnie, tried to perform a miracle here tonight? 'Well, it depends what you mean by a miracle.' So what is a miracle? Anybody like to answer?"

A lady three rows back took charge. "It's an event you cannot rationally explain," she said. "It seems logically impossible. It breaks the laws of nature. So some people would assume it must have been caused by God. As for your friend, I don't mind him trying to perform a miracle but on two provisos. First, that he doesn't claim to be the son of God if he succeeds. Second, that his miracle only involves collateral damage to my credulity and not to this building or any of us inside it."

Once the laughter had died down and Martelli had given the assurances requested she added, "The problem, of course, is with the laws of nature. We have only a provisional scientific understanding of them. One of my old tutors Jack Haldane was fond of saying, 'Science is as yet in its infancy, and we can foretell little of the future save that the thing that has not been is the thing that shall be; that no beliefs, no values, no institutions are safe.' If it is ever proved, as Big Bang theory suggests, that the universe really did begin fifteen billion years ago from the explosion of a singularity roughly the size of a chicken's egg then it would cease to enjoy the status of the miraculous, at least in my mind. You see we associate miracles exclusively with religious practice not scientific. But there is no reason why we should. To a scientist 'miraculous' is a derogatory term. It implies we have given up on the causal investigation.

"When I was younger the inexplicable and the impossible provided huge fodder for my imagination. I have witnessed a friend who was absolutely terrified of dentistry and all its needle-in-the-gums paraphernalia have two rotten teeth extracted painlessly while in a hypnotic state. I watched in amazement a hypnotized subject's arm swell up in gross purple blotches when it was suggested to him that he had brushed it against a deadly night-shade plant. How can these things happen? We are still miles away from understanding the mechanics of hypnotism in the same way we are miles away from understanding the mechanics of the placebo effect. I went to Brazil to try to find out the truth about their so-called psychic surgeons and came to the conclusion they are merely leger de main conjurors. I say 'merely' but there was no doubt that the best of them achieved significant post-op recovery rates and from patients suffering conditions that orthodox medicine had diagnosed terminal or untreatable.

"The common factor in all these and numerous other examples, I eventually concluded, was the patient's unquestioning trust in the ability and authority of the operative. Now we can argue about the ethical dimension of such activities and whether such complete surrender of one's critical faculty should be encouraged. But we cannot argue about the results because they defy all notions of statistical probability. Edgar Mitchell tells a story that illustrates the ability of a sincerely trusting mind to alter physical reality. His mother who was a committed Christian had gone virtually blind and all medical interventions to help her had been tried and failed. One day Edgar introduced her to a spiritual healer friend called Norbu and they hit it off famously. After several hours treatment involving trance meditation and chanting Mrs Mitchell was sent to bed. The next morning she proclaimed her sight was fully restored and to prove it she drove the long journey back to her home, something she had been unable to do for years. Several days later, having gone about her business without glasses and near perfect vision Mrs Mitchell rang her son wanting to know more about Norbu and his religious beliefs. Was he a Christian? She insisted she had to know. When Edgar reluctantly informed her he was a Tibetan Buddhist Mrs Mitchell's deep pain of regret became apparent in her voice. She had been treated by an instrument of evil and would not be dissuaded otherwise. Within hours her sight had deteriorated back to its original condition. Edgar comments that 'for several years he would continue to underestimate the power of belief in our lives because of the pervasiveness of my classical scientific training. My belief in the rationality of science,' he says, 'blinded me to the equally rational consequences of disbelief.'

"You may have noticed how often the terms 'religious' and 'spiritual' get used almost interchangeably. What, if any, is the difference between them? This is the kind of question that interested the pioneers of the new science of Psychology when it was taking off in the last quarter of the nineteenth century. When the subjects to whom research psychologists spoke claimed to have visions of angels or other celestial beings or to experience deep feelings of connectivity with the universe or to have their prayers for healing answered, what was really going on? One initial theory psychologists had was that these experiences were somehow being hypnotically self-induced. A kind of autosuggestion or concretised wishful thinking was in play. There took place many intriguing demonstrations and clinical analyses of hypnotism in that late Victorian epoch. As the century ended along came an American psychologist called William James who embarked on the massive academic project of amalgamating, studying and synthesising all the field and theoretical work his colleagues had been doing in these areas. His pedagogic summation is well worth considering.

"But before I come to James's conclusions about the veracity of religious experience I want to reference a Newsweek Beliefnet poll conducted in 2005. Statistically speaking the sample is quite small but I consider the data does reflect a reasonably accurate impression of where Americans stand in relation to the religious and spiritual debate. For instance 24%

defined themselves as spiritual but not religious while 55% as both spiritual and religious. When asked how important were their reasons for undertaking a religious/spiritual practice the same survey group replied as follows: 55% did so 'to connect with something larger than themselves', 70% 'to find happiness and peace of mind', 75% 'to forge a relationship with God', 63% 'to give their life meaning and structure', 38% 'to be part of a community', 75% 'to help them be a better person'. And all of these ticked 'very important' on a sliding 5 point scale that descended to 'not at all important' and 'don't know'.

"The outcomes of religious and spiritual practice may legitimately be described in terms of an increase in wellbeing and inner peace of mind and security for the practitioner. I suggest that a religious practice is something ritualised and authorised by a Church institution or doctrinal authority whereas a spiritual practice can be, and often is, almost any activity at all. When the Olympic gold medal winning sprinter, Eric Liddell, said, 'I believe God made me for a purpose. But he also made me fast. When I run I feel his pleasure,' he was inadvertently making this same point. I enjoyed running too when I was young and the exhilaration and sense of wellbeing I gained from this regular sporting activity saw me through what otherwise might have been some unbearably painful teenage years. Every dedicated sportsperson knows the psychological highs, the feeling of utter euphoria and personal empowerment that is obtained during performance. A sports psychologist called Tim Gallwey conducted the first serious studies of this phenomenon in a 1974 book entitled, *The Inner Game of Tennis*. Psychologists, however, had been discussing the nature of 'peak experiences' for quite a long time before that.

"Abraham Maslow, for instance, described peak experiences as 'self-validating, self-justifying moments with their own intrinsic value; never negative, unpleasant or evil; disoriented in time and space; and accompanied by a loss of fear, anxiety, doubts, and inhibitions'. Peak experiences were to me, and still remain so, sudden feelings of intense happiness and wellbeing, during which I gain an awareness of the existence of an Ultimate Truth and of the unifying reality of all things.

Accompanying these experiences is a heightened sense of control over my body and emotions, and a greater, more lucid percipience as though I was standing upon a mountaintop. If you have ever had a peak experience you will recall how replete you became with wonder and awe. One feels perfectly integrated with the world and creatively enlarged by it. Everything seems possible and one is aware without any doubt intruding that 'all things shall be well'.

"Now peak experiences do not only occur in the context of sport, of course. They occur in the context of all dedicated human activities. Another activity that potentially delivers peak experience to me personally is writing. Not always, of course, but when I am 'in the zone', to use Gallwey's term, the pages virtually write themselves smooth as silk while I seem to float omnisciently somewhere above the desk where my physical body labours. What are the activities that deliver peak experiences to you personally? I wonder. Have you recognized them yet? The bizarre truth about reality, at least inner psychological reality, is that it changes when we fully participate in it. What I mean by 'fully' is wholeheartedly, unstintingly, with all our attentive energy involved. In certain contexts and in certain individuals who often get categorized as 'mystics' or 'seers' this surfeit of undiluted attentive energy seems to endow their owners with unusual powers of intuition, prophecy and healing. Of course, such powers and such changes in reality cannot be measured in a laboratory and therefore their very existence tends to be disputed by a certain type of narrow scientific materialist.

"William James, the brother of Henry who you will know as a distinguished novelist, did not fall into that category. His book known as *The Varieties Of Religious Experience* is actually the text of a series of twenty lectures he delivered in 1902 at Edinburgh University. As I implied earlier, James' scholarship and rigorous analysis are unimpeachable as too is his secular scientific objectivity. He concludes that human nature contains a will and a need to believe in some higher power. The name of *faith state,* James says, is an entirely apposite one. 'It is a biological as well psychological condition, and Tolstoy is absolutely right in classing *faith* among the forces *by which men live.* The total absence of it, anhedonia, means collapse.' James goes on to cite J.H. Leuba, a colleague in the vanguard of the psychology of religion studies, as follows:

"'When, however, a positive intellectual content is imposed upon a faith state, it gets invincibly stamped in upon belief, and this explains the passionate loyalty of religious people everywhere to the minutest details of their so widely differing creeds. Taking creeds and faith state together, as forming religions, and treating these as purely objective phenomena without regard to their question of truth, we are obliged, on account of their extraordinary influence upon action and endurance, to class them among the most important biological functions known to mankind. Their stimulant and anaesthetic effect are so great....that as long as men can use their God they care very little who he is, or whether he is at all. The truth of the matter can be put in this way: God is not known, he is not understood, he is used – sometimes as a meat-purveyor, sometimes as moral support, sometimes as friend, sometimes as an object of love. If he proves himself useful the religious consciousness asks for no more than that. *Does God exist? How does he exist? What is he?* are so many irrelevant questions. Not God but life, more life, a larger richer more satisfying life, is, in the last analysis, the end of religion. The love of life, at any and every level of development, is the religious impulse.'"

Martelli took a sip of water and exchanged glances with Johnnie Woo who was sitting almost in a trance of concentration. "Well, so much for Psychology's opinion of religion and its faith-state. What about Science and its own 'faith state'? Does Science indeed have a faith state or does it as an epistemology exist above the ideological fray in an impenetrable and incontestable bubble of rationality? Well certainly this appears to be the case to a scientist who writes 'Faith is the great cop-out, the great excuse to evade the need to think and evaluate evidence. Faith is belief in spite of, even perhaps because of, the lack of evidence'. Of course Professor Dawkins' statement begs the crucial question 'what do we mean by evidence?' For a sociologist and psychologist 'evidence' takes a distinctly different form than it does for the Physicist, Chemist and Biologist, but the non laboratory testable evidence of social-psychology, I would argue, make no less a contribution to our better understanding of the human condition. However, when the same scientist writes, 'I am against religion because it teaches us to be satisfied with not understanding the world' he appears to make a more valid point. It is indisputable that much self-serving complacency does exist in religious circles and can be particularly characteristic of blinkered fundamentalist conceptions of religious belief.

"It occurs to me, however, that in contesting the legitimacy of *all* religious belief in this way Dawkins opens himself up to the counter allegation that hard empirical science 'teaches us to be satisfied with understanding the world as entirely reducible to its materially measurable component parts.' The scientific materialist author of *The Magic Of Reality* exhorts us, 'Next time you look in a mirror just think: that is what you are too,' namely, 'a survival machine for genes'. This dismisses at a stroke the whole idea of social, psychological and emotional becoming – and I use the word *becoming* with the same inflexion of meaning as Simone De Beauvoir uses it in *The Second Sex*: 'one is not born, but rather becomes, a woman'.

"Albert Einstein did not conceive of Science as being at loggerheads with religion but in a close relationship. He wrote, 'By way of the understanding he [the scientist] achieves a far-reaching emancipation from the shackles of personal hopes and desires, and thereby attains that humble attitude of mind towards the grandeur of reason incarnate in existence, and which, in its profoundest depths, is inaccessible to man. This attitude, however, appears to me to be religious, in the highest sense of the word. And so it seems to me that science not only purifies the religious impulse of the dross of its anthropomorphism but also contributes to a religious spiritualization of our understanding of life......My religion consists of a humble admiration of the illimitable superior Spirit who reveals himself in the slight details we are able to perceive with our frail and feeble minds. The deeply emotional conviction of the presence of a superior reasoning Power, which is revealed in the incomprehensible universe, forms my idea of God.'

"Such sentiments are supported amongst other scientists by the oncologist, Deepak Chopra, who asserts, 'In cultural terms science has now become easily the most credible of the religions,' while adding that, 'Science and religion are not really opposites but just very different ways of trying to decode the universe. Both visions contain the material world, which is a given. There has to be an unseen force of creation because the cosmos can be traced back only so far before time and space dissolve. And there has to be a place where the two opposites meet.' And John Polkinghorne, a latter day theoretical physicist, in his book, *Belief In God In An Age Of Science*, compares the doctrinal development of science with that of religion. The 'long and tangled tale of physics' he demonstrates 'exhibits features found in other quests for understanding'.

"Science is at bottom also a faith-state but it has been so successful and influential in its achievements that it can sometimes get carried away and forget this. Science is by no means immune to misconstruction and failure in its methodologies. The hostility and epistemic violence with which scientific materialists, particularly of the old school, treat religionists has been vitriolic in recent decades. And I hesitate to deny that certain fundamentalist targets have not deserved the onslaught of scientific rationalism. But here is the anomaly. Scientific rationalism itself stands on a quicksand of uncertainty and needs a strong foundation of faith to support it. This point was also well made by Einstein when answering a letter from a schoolboy who asked him if scientists prayed:

"'I have tried to respond to your question as simply as I could. Here is my answer,' wrote Einstein. 'Scientific research is based on the idea that everything that takes place is deter-mined by laws of nature, and therefore this holds for the actions of people. For this reason, a research scientist will hardly be inclined to believe that events could be influenced by prayer, i.e. by a wish addressed to a supernatu-ral being. However, it must be admitted that our actual knowledge of these laws is only imperfect and fragmentary, so that, actually the belief in the existence of basic all-embracing laws in nature also rests on a sort of faith. All the same this faith has been largely justified so far by the success of scientific research. But, on the other hand, everyone who is seriously involved in the pursuit of science becomes convinced that a spirit is manifest in the laws of the Universe - a spirit vastly superior to that of man, and one in the face of which we with our modest powers must feel humble. In this way the pursuit of science leads to a religious feeling of a special sort, which is indeed quite different from the religiosity of someone more naive.'

Martelli paused to lubricate her mouth. "Other scientists I know would press the point much further, of course," she continued. "*What validates the supremacy of analytical reason apart from analytical reason itself?* is a tautological question sometimes expressed. And *whose* reason is it, anyway? Men's or women's? Well, I don't want to diverge more than I need to into gender politics tonight, if you will forgive me, and anyway I intend to hand over now to our putative miracle worker and see what he 's cooked up."

Johnnie stood up and walked to the micro-phone. "I'd like to make a prediction. Now please do not give yourself away if this is true of you," he said. "My prediction is that someone in this room celebrates their birthday on September 17."

Hardly a face flickered and Martelli took over. "That is not much of a prediction, I can sense you saying to yourselves," she smiled. "And you would be right. I calculate the probability of our clairvoyant being accurate is no better than one in three, perhaps a little less. Now what do you think the probability would be of Johnnie tapping the person who has that birthday, if there is such a person, on the shoulder?" A few guesses were called out during which Johnnie made his way down the central aisle. When he eventually stopped he pointed at an elderly man and said, "I'm sorry I am physically unable to reach your shoulder, sir, but I am nominating you. Yes, you sir. Does your birthday fall on September 17?"

The man's face split into an incredulous grin as he affirmed the accuracy of Johnnie's prediction. "Would you please pass me something that belongs to you - a handkerchief, a wallet, a watch perhaps?" the man was asked. In return Johnnie received a wristwatch and he rubbed it gently between his fingers while closing his eyes. After about half a minute Johnnie said, "I feel you were born in 1921 and you were a pilot at a battle somewhere in Holland. Arnhem is the name I can hear. Your plane was brought down and you became a prisoner of war. You have the George Cross and, let me see, you have been attending a Unitarian church since 1959 to which you were introduced by your late wife, Clare."

Once the gentleman had recomposed himself, the clapping died down and Johnnie had returned to his seat Martelli said, "Right, do you have any questions, please?" A man she vaguely recognised stood up as if to speak but he walked towards the exit door instead, extracting a mobile from his pocket. Once outside he made the call. "Your hunch was right, Weller," he said. "He arrived here with Martelli a short while ago. What?....Can't say for certain. I'll tail them when they leave and confirm....Yeah, she spouted a load of mumbo jumbo and he did some kind of ham fisted mind reading act....Right. Let's just say Paul McKenna aint got nothing to worry about!"

LIFE AND DEATH

**18** Edgar Laidlaw awoke dripping with the sweat of terror and his bedroom gradually shaped into lopsided reality. Thank God the place was intact! The conflagration scorching his consciousness had been but a dream; yet so pungent the stench of roasting flesh as he held Donna in his embrace that the engulfing flames still choked his nostrils. Tumbling out of bed he doused his clammy body in a shower of cold water then switched on the radio, seeking the anodyne comfort of greater London chatter. "Police believe the missing schoolgirl, Donna Atkinson, may be held in a cellar somewhere on the 243 London bus route," he heard instead. "A search is in progress and the public are requested – " But that was as far as it went. Laidlaw's fist thumped the broadcast into crackling silence.

Downstairs in the dungeon that had now served as her domicile for a week Donna heard a clatter of footsteps approaching from the outside road and rushed to the tiny window shouting for help. Above her a pair of black shoes crossed in and then out of the attenuated frame of her vision. "Please help me! I'm imprisoned down here!" she yelled but the words merely bounced round the walls of the coffin utterly unheard and not for the first time she dropped on the mattress sobbing with despair.

"I've had all the sketches you've completed framed," announced Laidlaw when he arrived forty minutes later carrying a breakfast tray. "I'm going out now to collect them. Have you further considered my proposal?" His smile of encouragement was not reciprocated. "You shall of course be handsomely remunerated. Love is friendship and admiration that have caught fire," he remarked as he departed, "and love is what I feel for you, Donna."

Sarah and Mike were in morning parley at the Atkinson home. "I don't trust the police, even though they've eventually pulled their finger out," she was saying. "They keep grilling me about The Unreasonable Club. They think I'm a militant troublemaker but can't classify what sort. We can't just sit back and leave it to them." A text arrived from Joanne Cunningham wanting to see Sarah urgently. *Sorry, too busy right now*, she messaged back.

Mike had developed several new theories. Perhaps Donna's captor had an amorous fixation and was waiting for it to be returned – 'Stockholm Syndrome' as it is known in the psychiatric trade or 'traumatic bonding'? "Perhaps you've been reading too many text books," was Sarah's ironic reply. Perhaps the 243 bus was on diversion the day Donna spotted it? "That sounds less Hollywood," considered Sarah. They mulled it over and Mike made a call to London Buses Customer Service who directed him elsewhere to a depot. By 10.30 he was driving east to investigate the hypothesis further.

The gut-wrenching foreboding Laidlaw had woken with recurred as he parked near the High Street. The mug-shot of Donna stared back at him from every shop window and the police were randomly interviewing pedestrians. "No, I'm sorry, I don't recognise her," he responded to a constable who followed him into the picture framing shop. "But I pray you find her very soon." The officer assured Laidlaw the police net was tightening and Donna's discovery imminent. "How the hell did they get on the scent?" he anguished. "It's just bluster. I must hold my nerve." But once back in the car his bravado disintegrated. He knew he needed a plan B, an exit strategy, and drove directly to a petrol station.

On the dot of 1pm Sinclair Scott lurched into Williamson's consultancy. He wore a ruffled cream suit and the stink of booze hung around him like fog. "I'm not expecting a freebie, Martin," the Australian actor slurred, dropping uninvited into a chair. "I've already paid your Sheila the going rate. I've been feeling very anxious lately. I've been thinking about death all the time. First, my neighbour croaks. One day he's cracking jokes, cleaning his car, next day major heart attack and he's worm fodder. Second, that Atkinson girl's hustling me. Don's kid. She knows what we did to her dad. She's talking to the Bill. We're all gonna end up rotting behind bars!"

"What we *tried* to do," corrected Williamson. "We didn't succeed. And Don's kid is winding you up. Take a few deep breaths and try to relax. She knows absolutely nothing."

"So you keep insisting, mate," countered Scott, "but I never saw my share of the contract money again! We were evil bastards the three of us. What insane demon jinxed us? Who the hell were we way back then anyway? When the plods knock on my door I've decided to confess everything." Williamson said nothing. He wanted to punch the whinging Australian and Scott seemed to sense it. "Weller and me played you like a gilded harp," Scott taunted back. "You ached for Margaret and you wore your pain so sanctimoniously. Me, I hated Don's talent, his charm, his looks, his versatility and most of all the way the birds admired him. People like Don didn't deserve to live, at least not in the same miserable world I inhabited. But you, Marty, being a philanthropic student of human nature, you hypocrite, you had to believe your actions were noble."

Williamson composed himself and asked, "So what exactly is it you require this student of human nature to do for you?"

Scott's eyes shifted and blurred out of lachrymose focus as he gulped pitifully for air. "If there's an afterlife I'm going to finish up being char-grilled for eternity in Hell's flames," he moaned and wiped a bit of imaginary grit from his left eye. "Unless you can somehow absolve me," he pleaded. "You know, mate, put me back on side with God and all that?"

"What's he doing?" Donna wondered. For several hours the ceiling had reverberated footsteps punctuated by scrapes and thuds as if Laidlaw was rearranging the furniture. When he eventually deigned to descend that evening with food an acrid smell accompanied him. "I need a shower," she said timorously but he morosely shook his head and retreated. Whenever he accompanied her to the bathroom on the upper floor it was locked from the outside. Perhaps the thinly panelled door could be kicked down, once he was out of earshot? she several times had fantasised. Nearby on the landing a wall-ladder seemed to give access to a loft. Perhaps an escape could be somehow contrived through the roof? "If only I was braver!" she cursed herself. "I'm such a pathetic coward!"

The following morning as Mike ferreted the car through tedious gridlocks he urged his companion to inform the police. A bus company official had confirmed that the day Donna disappeared the 243 had been put on diversion due to emergency road-works and he had even supplied the relevant re-routing detail. Sarah shook her head. "If the psychos who've got Donna even smell a copper closing in they might kill her and dump the body," she insisted. "This has to be our job." And she stared at the street map of Stoke Newington for which they remained remorselessly headed.

"You've got 15 minutes," said Laidlaw locking Donna into the bathroom for her daily ablution. The stink of petrol had irritated her nostrils all night and had become far more pervasive as she was frogmarched up the cellar stairs and passed through the ground floor. Although he had placed a bag over her head Donna divined what sort of atrocity was being perpetrated and its very invisibility terrified her. Laidlaw must have created an inflammable barricade to deter intruders!

A hundred yards due north Mike parked the car outside a long terrace of insalubrious housing. "68, 66! This way quick!" shouted Sarah running ahead. When he caught up with her she was standing opposite a number 40, biting her lips. "It might not be this one," cautioned Mike, eyeing the bay windows, peeling white paint, drawn curtains, low garden wall and beyond it concrete steps down to a basement. Sarah moved forward alone and pushed open the gate. And within an instant she was down below street level peering at a scrap of paper wedged in the solitary window. It contained the word BOOMERANG. "What are you doing?" demanded Sarah rapidly re-ascending the steps. But it was too late. Mike had already alerted the police on his mobile.

Laidlaw spotted them immediately from a vantage point upstairs, a screaming posse of red and blue vehicles. Momentarily shuddering beneath the psychic boom of his fate, he sprinted downstairs to ignite the huge funeral pyres built out of furniture and whatever other materials had come to hand. Whoosh, whoosh, whoosh! sang the bonfires leaping into frantic life and the roar rose like Wagnerian thunder as Laidlaw scrambled to attend to his captive.

Outside panic had set in amongst the rapidly gathering crowd. Two officers on the point of forcing entry had been hurled brutally back by the fireball and lay in charcoal tatters on the road. Others physically restrained Sarah from entering the conflagration. Adjacent homes outpoured residents. A flat-capped inspector bawled electronic instructions for the fire brigade to be dispatched.

Laidlaw meanwhile, having heard Donna shoulder-charging the bathroom door, confronted her with a diabolical request to join him in a suicide pact as he opened it up. "Life and death are both impostors. They mock us, Donna, and we should treat them equally the same. Take this cyanide capsule and lie down with me in the rear bedroom," he coaxed. "There is no escape. Our passing shall be painless and we shall be united in a state of eternal cosmic innocence." She preceded him obediently into the room, took the pill from his hand then suddenly, involuntarily brought her knee hard up into his groin. Instantaneously out again, yanking the attic ladder from its mooring and scrambling towards the ceiling hatch.

"Donna! Come back!" she heard beneath her as she clattered it open and forced her quaking body through the aperture. As she groped around the murky joists suddenly the voice piped up again but this time much closer. The madman's contorted face appeared and she instinctively lashed out with her feet. "Please! Please, Donna! I beg you!" she heard against the cackle of advancing flames. "Not like this!"

"He's not human. He's a monster," she kept telling herself as she stamped repeatedly on the bulbous growth until finally, in a cacophony of bestial howls, Edgar Laidlaw plummeted back down the chute into smoky oblivion.

Johnnie Woo felt deeply honoured as well as sorely afraid. Martelli trusted him implicitly. Why else would she leave him in sole charge of her home while she went off on a half-term jaunt with her great grandchild? "You'll be totally safe from Weller living here," she encouraged in response to Johnnie's insistence that Weller's ruthless malice and deviousness knew no bounds. "Go through these dvds while I'm out. They demonstrate the work of our organisation more fully. There is no trick photography. Forget the likes of Derren Brown and Dynamo. What you will see is berated as occult phenomena in vulgar parlance. We, the people of the veil, call it reality. And don't open the door to anyone. Alright?"

Five days had passed but the tabloids were still full of it. Donna had become box office. One paper had offered her £300,000 for the exclusive publishing rights to her story of captivity and liberation. *"The great escape artist speaks only to us!"* shrieked a Daily Mail headline. Sarah muttered with disapproval until Donna explained, "I'm giving you half the money, as well as my fee for appearing on The Jonathan Ross show."

What indemnified Donna's status of celebrity was that her escape from the house fire had been caught on camera and enjoyed ten million YouTube viewings already. The burgeoning conflagration, the female head emerging through a skylight, the teetering vertiginous rooftop walk, the firemen swinging their mechanical ladder into position and the final daredevil leap into salvation's arms. "It reminds me of a gap in a row of teeth after an extraction," remarked Mike when they revisited the residential terrace. Nothing left but scorched rubble and damp ashes where Laidlaw had once plied his lonely aesthetic trade.

It was an impassive and carefully enunciated voice message but the sense cut through Williamson's suave professional demeanour like jagged glass. "Joanne has told me all about your sex games and your pillow talk confessions. You will know Joanne better as Margaret. The games are now over and the executioner's axe hovers over your head. You have 48 hours to give me the fully unexpurgated account of your relationship with my mother and father. Failure to supply it will propel me to the police and the Neuropsychiatry Association. Your career will be forthwith terminated unless I decide you have some credible explanation, you lying evil fornicating scumbag." And what traumatised the listener most was the calm matter-of-fact way in which Sarah uttered those final four words.

Johnnie watched Martelli's dvds in a state of astounding lucid confusion. Here in technicolour close-up detail were all the gospel miracles then some! The peasant walking on water was viewed simultaneously by cameras beneath and above the sea. The cadaver pronounced clinically dead by a senior oncologist spontaneously revived as a white-robed figure sprinkled blossoms over it. On being given water to sip, this latter day Lazarus proceeded to describe in accurate detail the hospital rooms through which his ethereal body had just previously been floating.

To Donna Jonathan Ross had seemed as amicable and wise-guy witty in real life as he did on the telly. He had graciously thanked her for allowing him to have a preliminary chat. In reply to Ross's questions Donna explained, "Mr Laidlaw talked continuously while I sketched him. A lot of it went over my head. There were so many long unintelligible words. I felt like a priest must do taking confession from a boffin. After about three days he started to tell me he loved me. No sexual advances though. Not one." Ross had looked disappointed at this.

"Appawently Laidlaw allowed you to send a coded text message to your sister in which you asked her to feed your pet cat called Boomer-wang," lisped Ross. "Can you tell us how that came about? Funny name for a cat!"

"I don't have a cat," laughed Donna. "That's what I told him. He wanted me to do drawings and I told him I'd only cooperate if he let me phone my sister, Sarah. 'Out of the question!' he said and so we had this stand-off until he relented and let me send her a text instead. Of course he monitored what I wrote before allowing it to go."

Ross asked Donna about the background to the code games she played with Sarah then once the subject was exhausted tried to encourage her to expound on her own trepidation and suffering as Laidlaw's captive. "To be honest I only got really scared when I smelled the petrol," she replied. "Before that, even though I felt powerless and abused, I still felt I had some degree of control over the situation. It would end soon. You see, he was very polite and asked me what I wanted to eat, that sort of thing. 'True artists are sacred and above reproach', Mr Laidlaw used to say. And he included me in that community. I pretty quickly realised I was sort of his object of worship as well as his prisoner. 'Humanity is utterly loathsome in its selfishness and ignorance', he'd insist. 'Humanity is rushing headlong to extinction and only the artists can redeem the situation'. I'd just nod my head and ask, 'May I take a shower now please?'"

The second dvd Johnnie played was called *Sanity, Madness and Ignorance: A Brief history.* Lots of talking heads, often on ancient film stock, analysed the human dilemma. Warfare received especially short shrift, particularly the 20th century world wars which were envisaged as the consequence of institutionalised collective insanity. Psychopathic megalomaniacs colluding with or revolting against each other's power drunk delusions. A grainy monochrome Albert Einstein cryptically commented, "Few are those who see with their own eyes and feel with their own hearts. A man should look for what is and not for what he thinks should be. Common sense is the collection of prejudices acquired by age eighteen."

The senior clinical partner was eleven years younger than Williamson and much smarter, two facts that Williamson sullenly resented. "David, I've been wondering if that early retirement package you offered me last March is still available?" he smiled synthetically to his colleague over lunch. David studied the other assiduously. He had wanted rid of Williamson for ages considering him privately as a third rate analyst yet the practice was worth millions and the monetary reconciliation had to be right. What, David wondered, had changed the man's mind? "It's just recently I've become exceptionally aware of Time's winged chariot," replied Williamson, "and there are a few things I want to do, places I'd like to visit, before the deserts of vast eternity catch up with me." Then he added pointedly, "But I'll take the deal only on condition that we can complete the paperwork in the next 48 hours."

The third dvd Johnnie played was called *A New Model Of Reality* and featured a younger version of Martelli and a man she introduced as her colleague, Don Atkinson. "What we materially construe as reality is an illusion," opined Don, "albeit a very persistent one. My first great childhood influence was William Blake who wrote about human consciousness in terms of 'mind forged manacles', the conceptual rigidity that traps us in a three dimensional material world. 'If the doors of perception were cleansed,' said Blake, 'every thing would appear to man as it is, Infinite. For man has closed himself up, till he sees all things thro' narrow chinks of his cavern.' Let us take a closer look at what Blake meant...."

The explanation was no more that 15 minutes in when Johnnie's mobile rang. "Mr Woo? I'm Charles Fothergill and I work for Harrod's in the customer services department," he heard. It was a refined upper class voice. "We were given your number by Professor Martelli," Fothergill explained. "She's having a toy delivered that she's just purchased, sir. It's quite large." Johnnie explained he was under strict instructions not to open the door to anyone. "Yes, she told us that, sir," responded the caller. "Our delivery man will leave it in the front porch for you to collect when you will. He should be there about 3pm."

The distinctive green Harrod's vehicle pulled up right on time. From his vantage point upstairs Johnnie watched the driver alight stiffly and cross towards the house carrying a box shaped object. He wore a smart uniform and white gloves. After the van had departed Johnnie hesitated, nervously wondering what to do. Then he put a call through to Martelli but it instantly went into call minder mode. "I've become bloody paranoid," he cursed himself as he descended to the front door. The large oblong parcel was wrapped in brown paper, neatly embossed with Harrods stickers and a brief personal message in what appeared to be Martelli's own hand informing him where to place it in the house. He lifted it up carefully and banged the door shut behind him with a foot.

"There are multiple different types of conscious-ness," Don was explaining as the dvd resumed later, "and not just waking, sleeping and dreaming as classical science tends to insist. The varieties of 'bliss consciousness' for instance are at least five-fold, - inspired by beauty, love, physical exertion, Samadhi, and problem resolution. Bliss interacts with the observable world and transforms it. Together with its antithesis 'pain consciousness,' bliss demonstrates the mutability and relative nature of all our sensory experience. As Einstein noted, 'When you are courting a nice girl an hour seems like a second. When you sit on a red-hot cinder a second seems like an hour. That's relativity'."

It was deep stuff and thought provoking enough for Johnnie not to notice how much his hands had begun to itch. Suddenly he gazed at them with alarm. Red blotches and contusions had begun to form on his fingers and palms and he rushed to the bathroom to bathe them. The cold sudsy water offered instant relief but it did not last long. Once back in the viewing room the itching returned and when a text came through on his mobile the pain spread instantly to the rest of his body. *Goodbye, sucker!* Johnnie read. *You are now a dead man walking.*

DARKNESS AND LIGHT

Sarah lay in bed idly listening to Radio 4 and intermittently wondering how to spend £150,000. Some of the money, she felt, she ought to give to Joanne, who no longer had a job in Belgravia, having handed in her resignation after anonymously tipping off the police about what went on there. The vice squad had taken the allegation seriously. On its own, of course, such un-sourced information would not have necessarily meant too much but it exactly supported a more detailed deposition submitted by a middle ranking Metropolitan police officer two days earlier.

Suddenly the signal on Sarah's portable bedside radio seemed to fade and another programme momentarily supplanted it as if some invisible airwaves controller had accidentally crossed the wires. And the brief displacements continued at intermittent intervals thereafter. The effect eerily jogged her memory and sent her scurrying for her father's journals.

Christopher La Frayne was relaxing in his marble bath when the butler called through the door, "Sir, two policemen are here!" La Frayne sipped his coffee and instructed the menial to tell them he was indisposed. "They refuse to leave, sir," replied the man. "They asked me to inform you they have interviewed Madame Lucinda and she is now under arrest!"

The passage Sarah had suddenly been prompted to recall was duly located in one of Don's earliest notebooks and she re-read it avidly: *Fina says that spiritual reality initially breaks through our sensibility in brief unexpected episodes, a bit like a pirate radio station usurping the frequency of its closest established neighbour. As the initiate grows in spiritual attentiveness he hears more of the pirate transmission and less of the established one. A new reality awareness is born. The darkness of the mundane and temporal is displaced by the light of the unique and ethereal. And it is this transcendent level of awareness that the people of the veil have attained through disciplined practice. There are carefully coded passages in the Gnostic gospels that refer to this phenomenon. Fina insists that we have all become the prisoners of Cartesian duality. We are indoctrinated from childhood in a convention of rational analytical duality that renders our sensibility arid and myopic and parsimonious. To the spiritually enlightened people of the veil what our fallen world calls 'the miraculous' has become entirely normative. Ask and it shall be given to you.* Sarah stopped reading. "Who the hell is this Fina?" she anguished.

Ariana was Martelli's most trusted colleague in the UK. Johnnie Woo gazed at her forlornly now as he shifted in and out of sleep consciousness. "Where is Professor Martelli?" he wanted to ask but his larynx failed him. "Fina has gone to Sussex University to give a lecture," said Ariana as if hearing him telepathically. Her voice so tender and loving permeated Johnnie's being. "No, Johnnie, you are going to live a long productive life," she continued as if in answer to his next question. "The balm I have massaged into your hands and arms is working just great. It was made in Tibet from a secret formula of rare plant extracts. The Dalai Lama used it to cure himself of a malignant cancer. Close your eyes and rest now."

Outside the lecture theatre Martelli's book, *Heaven And Earth,* was selling like hot cakes. The departments of Psychology, Social Science and Anthropology had all placed it on recommended reading lists. Mike arrived early with Donna and browsed through the index. Nearby in the staff common room Martelli spoke to Ariana on the phone. "If he deteriorates summon Isaac Jacobsen immediately," she advised. "Isaac is 75% sure the strychnine and dimethyl-mercury solution they treated the paper packaging with would not in itself kill Johnnie. Weller is relying on the nocebo effect. He knows Johnnie is very superstitious, one of his friends died after receiving a shaman's curse in Mexico. You have to purge Johnnie's consciousness of the toxic anxiety Weller has placed there, then Johnnie's mind will effect the cure itself. I don't need to remind you of all people, Ariana, that words properly constructed and delivered have magical properties. They rekindle the embers of hope into a fire of redemption."

Ten hours in police custody had not dented one iota La Frayne's façade of indignant innocence. Now his brief, Gareth Stirling, one of the capital's smartest and most expensive, had gone into private parley with the vice squad. A wisp of a smile played on Stirling's lips as he returned to tell his client, "They don't want you. They want the procurer. Supply the name and you will be given the lesser charge of keeping a bawdy house. We can fight that in the same way that newspaper crew are fighting the phone hacking charges." La Frayne's eyes narrowed. "But if I admit to knowing who procures the girls," he replied, "I'm implicitly as guilty as him?" Stirling shook his head and whispered, "So far as you understood, Chris, the girls would be working as legitimate nightclub hostesses. Isn't that what the invoices declare?"

"Almost four centuries ago in *Paradise Lost* John Milton wrote prophetically, "The mind is its own place and in itself, can make a Heaven of Hell, a Hell of Heaven," began Martelli. "The question I wish to consider today is 'how come in this post-scientific, post-nuclear age of immense technological achievement we still fail to grasp just how stupendously powerful the human mind is to penetrate and transform reality?' I mean social and interpersonal reality as much as anything. How come we remain so institutionally racist, sexist, destructive and materialistic? How come we allow the richest 65 individuals in the world to own as much wealth as the poorest three and half billion put together? Why do we privilege analytical logic above compassion and feeling? Corporate competition above communitarian socialism? Cynicism and doubt above hope and faith?

"When my friend the astrophysicist Edgar Mitchell was returning from the moon on the Apollo 14 he experienced an overwhelming sense of universal connectedness, an ecstasy of unity. It struck him powerfully that his presence as a space traveller and the existence of the universe itself was not accidental and that a highly intelligent cosmic process was at work. He perceived the universe as conscious. Such epiphanies are real. We are all capable of having them then later disowning the experience because they so fundamentally challenge our rational learnt convention of normality. Mitchell, until then a devout materialist, did not disown it, however. He set up *The Institute of Noetic Science* to resolve the complex insights acquired in space. If the universe is conscious it may well be, he concluded, the entity we call the Self could exist independently of its own physicality. Not the ego self, of course, the false front we wear to negotiate public reality. Mitchell meant the inner or soul self, that pure repository of awareness and potentiality that neither judges nor fears but simply delights, - the enlightened spiritual self that Julian of Norwich inhabits when she reassures us, *All shall be well, and all manner of things shall be well.*"

When Johnnie awoke from a bilious dream the image of Martelli surfaced with him. She appeared to be a child and dancing wildly with her parents at a party. Round and round they all whirled in hilarious circles! *Feena!* somebody shouted. *You will make us all sick! Feena!* But now Johnnie's eyelids opened on Ariana. "Why is Professor Martelli called Feena?" he whispered in confusion. "Oh, it was her family name," explained the kindly nurse. "You see, her middle name was Josefina and her parents simply shortened it to Fina."

"The vast majority of us possess wonderful spiritual gifts that just lie dormant and unrecognised," continued Martelli. "The great narcissistic organism called Society has little use for creative enlightenment. It demands a race of compliant robotic pawns to propagate its dark material purposes and the result on an individual level is accumulative spiritual entropy and mental disorder. As my colleague Erich Fromm wrote in his book *The Sane Society*, 'Mental health is characterised by the ability to love and to create, by the emergence from incestuous ties to clan and soil, by a sense of identity based on one's experience of self as the subject and agent of one's powers' - and that is what all the 'awakened ones,' the great spiritual leaders from Akhenaten and Lao-Tse to Socrates and Jesus unilaterally assert. 'Mental health cannot be defined in terms of the adjustment of the individual to his society but on the contrary in terms of the adjustment of society to the needs of man.'

"And one of the most basic needs of man, I'd argue, is to be hopeful. Hope is not equivalent to the canned laughter and applause manufactured by television companies to kid an audience into believing the lack lustre show they are watching must be good. Hope is an innate part of our species being. It is our psychic life-blood. As Lisel Mueller says in her poem of the same name, hope 'is the mouth that inflates the lungs of the child that has just been born', hope 'is the singular gift we cannot destroy in ourselves', hope 'is the genius that invents the future', hope 'is all we know of God'."

Donna was no intellectual but she understood enough of this and began to silently sob. Later, after Mike had queued to get Martelli to sign his copy of *Heaven and Earth,* Donna confided to him in the bar that Laidlaw had loomed large in her mind as Martelli spoke about the alienation tantamount to insanity of socialised humanity. "Mr Laidlaw was not really a bad man," she wept. "I think he just felt thwarted and frustrated in every area of his life."

"Look at this signature," said Mike who was proudly examining his new possession. "She's signed it *Fina* Martelli not Barbara. I'd better ring Sarah straightaway. It may be just a coincidence." Donna took a look. Fina? Barbara? So what? She didn't understand. "In your dad's notebooks," explained Mike taking out his mobile. "The name Fina keeps cropping up. She told me about her frustration in not being able to trace who or what it referred to." Donna still looked blank. "Oh, don't worry," smiled Mike. "You were busy sunning yourself in a cellar at the time of our conversation."

When at 9pm Williamson logged onto his Internet current account and saw the seven fat juicy digits, he almost purred with contentment. His partner David had delivered as promised. Williamson was out, - shot-proof and rich. Soon after that the doorbell rang and he answered it, oozing affability. Two plain-clothes policemen introduced themselves. "If this is about that raid at the club in Belgravia I know absolutely nothing – " Williamson began.

"It's not, sir," frowned the senior detective censoriously. "It's about Gregor Pidolski." Williamson gestured incomprehension. "Pidolski alleges you paid him £10,000 eighteen years ago to murder one Donald Atkinson. Can we come in please?"

 Once Mike had spoken to her about his copy of *Heaven and Earth* signed 'Fina Martelli' Sarah instantly emailed the author and received a phone call and warm recognition by return. "For organisational reasons my anonymity could not be jeopardised," Martelli confided. "But I'd ardently hoped you'd eventually get on to me." And an invitation to Fina's Islington home where Johnnie remained convalescing followed hard upon.

"Whatever complex thing consciousness may be," Martelli explained to Sarah over lunch, "to reduce the phenomenon merely to the firing of neurons in the brain, which is what scientific materialists do, is simply absurd. Institutionalised religion is no less obstructive to the truth with its asinine claims of a Daddy God offering eternal Pie-in-the-Sky happiness to the blindly obedient and worshipful, constructing salvation as a commodity assigned to the faithful. We may call the offer orthodox theisms make to their believers 'spiritual materialism'. And it is because these two materialisms of Science and Theism so dominate the global culture that 'the people of the veil' have had to remain underground, to avoid ideological contamination. Isaac Newton needed to keep his work on Alchemy secret to avoid being prosecuted for heresy. It's the same with us. We can take the public discourse only so far. Okay, today heresy laws don't exist in the same draconian way they historically did, but step out of ideological line and you get slapped down pretty damn fast. Modern systems of punishment for transgression are based on peer group ridicule and the withholding of research grants." The study door opened and Martelli turned round. "Oh, here comes Johnnie. I understand you two are already acquainted?"

"I gather you've been through the mill," Sarah said embracing Johnnie who, apart from a sallow pastiness, looked remarkably animated. "Fina's been telling me about my dad's contribution to the organisation. Apparently all 25,000 members have a code name. My dad's was Boomerang. What's yours?"

"Owl," answered Fina. "To whit to woo. Okay?" Sarah chuckled as she caught on. "Albert Einstein's was 'Slippers'. Gandhi's was 'Skinny'. Anthony Orwell's is '1984'." continued Fina. Johnnie sat down and encouraged Fina to carry on with what she had been originally saying. "Anyway, one of the main things the veil is trying to do is create a synthesis between two stubbornly diverse discourses, the scientific and the spiritual, weaving the best practices together. As Slippers once wrote, 'Science without religion is lame. Religion without science is blind.' Our task is to challenge and to filter out dogmas and false certainties from whatever epistemologies they exist in. And to that end we have people situated in all the major academic disciplines, additionally in the arts, the media, the law, politics, corporate business and even in the police force and army. They are seed corn agents of infrastructural change, a guerrilla force, whose first allegiance is to 'the people of the veil'. Sarah, before I speak further I need to know definitely that you want to be one of us?" After Sarah's enthusiastic affirmation, Fina said, "Excellent! It was your father's dearest wish. And now he will address you personally."

Martin Williamson disconsolately killed the television news images of Richard Weller being shoved into a police car then opened *Heaven and Earth* with the lugubrious solemnity of a bishop about to peruse the pulpit bible. Here the analyst reposed, several days into a lucrative retirement, a million plus pounds in the bank, yet only the bleakest sense of foreboding prevailed. It had always been like this, he reflected, a disconnection between his thoughts and his feelings, his head and his heart. Of course episodes redolent with optimism had intermittently occurred on the path of life, joyful illuminations of tedium, but nothing had ever been sustained for long. No relationship. No commitment. No progeny. No authentic creativity. "No intuitive sense of the divine", as the author of *Heaven and Earth* put it.

Williamson felt himself sinking into an invisible lacuna. He was lost to life, waiting for – what exactly? The custodial tap on the shoulder? It had just happened to Richard Weller, arrested at Heathrow while trying to flee the country in disguise with a false passport. And the ultimate absurdity, the man they had hired to kill Don

Atkinson almost two decades ago had converted to Christianity while serving a prison sentence for GBH and, as a matter of redemptive duty, had confessed to all his long list of historical misdemenours! Of course Williamson had denied everything to the police but the CPS had been briefed and Williamson bailed to await their decision on whether to prosecute. He could not fool himself. Retrospective justice in legal establishment circles was massively in fashion.

Sarah trembled to witness the reanimated image of her father. "My darling daughter, if you are watching this two things have happened," Don began. "I am dead and Fina has inducted you into the organisation. Wherever my soul resides and in whatever form, it will be immensely gratified and blessed. From early infancy your curiosity and percipience astonished me. The questions you bombarded us with! 'Daddy, what lives beyond the stars? Daddy, what makes my dreams happen? Daddy, why is the grass so green?' Adult convention inhibits our asking such fundamental questions, fear of being regarded as naïve and stupid. Of course we shall never know all the answers, at least not with our heads, intellectually. But as we grow spiritually the answers become available through the outpouring of the heart in gratitude and love, through the obliteration of the ego self, through a burgeoning trust in the benevolence of Providence; and we become touched in every cell of our being by the ecstasy of unity. Few are prepared to transcend the material dimension in this way and my dear friend, Fina, has judged you, Sarah, can be one of them."

Williamson was mortifying himself with the aid of the penultimate section of *Heaven and Earth* in which Martelli describes our human experience of reality "on the other side of the ego, where the monologue of the mind is perfectly stilled, where consciousness is qualitatively different. It is in that place alone enlightenment occurs," the passage continues. "In that place we do not have to seek personal power or self-validation because we have it in more than abundance. The will to *power* is a characteristic of ego consciousness and absolutely contrary to the will to enlightenment. But how many men can resist the call to behave *powerfully*? To be noticed, to be obeyed, to be the cause of fear in others, to be the teacher and not the taught – these attributes define masculine identity and without them a man is diminished, is rendered ineffectual and womanly in his own eyes. The more inadequate a man privately experiences himself to be, the more aggressively and cunningly and jealously he endeavours to reassert himself. Now such aggression is, of course, internally disguised and disowned. The fault is never his. The fault always belongs to the powerful *other*, whose power is rationalised as tyranny and arrogance, and this rationalisation can weigh heavily, causing him to covet whatever his enemy possesses, causing him to want to obliterate the enemy. And this blind mad craving to obliterate the enemy can even blossom over time into an act of legitimate moral duty."

"The people of the veil have their roots in Gnostic Christianity," Don was elaborating. "They are organically linked with Sufism and other progressive esoteric movements Fina will tell you about. I met Fina through her daughter, Penny, my first steady British girl-friend. Back then I was wrestling with issues related to my sexual orientation and, in my eventual realisation of who I authentically was, Fina became a crucial catalyst. You can trust her implicitly. You will meet many others whose gifts will astonish you, Sarah. My ardent hope is that your own evolving gifts will reciprocally astonish them too. The survival of humanity depends on our community of the esoterically gifted."

As he turned the page Williamson read, "We are supposed to be living in the age of *the new man*, an exotic calibre of being invented around 1980, held to be caring, sensitive, non-aggressive and entirely different to his emotionally obtuse dad. This paragon cleans the home, changes nappies and does the weekly shop at Waitrose. But has anything really fundamentally changed in the dark recesses of the male psyche? After all, violence within whichever social or geopolitical context we care to look is not abating. Do we see this new man in Afghanistan, Iraq, Darfur, Gaza, Syria or the other numerous trouble spots of the world? Do we see him in the SAS, the Marines, in Al Qaeda, the Taliban and ISIS? I suggest this new man, if not quite an invention of the marketing industry, was summarily appropriated by it and drained of virtually all his radical potential.

"Should we therefore feel everything is hopeless, that collective enlightenment is a pipe-dream, that the human lot must inevitably always be ignorance and self-deception and patriarchal? Common sense tells me yes, intuition and instinct tell me no. Enlightenment is the corollary of peace of mind. And peace of mind is a biological requirement as essential as fresh air and water to our survival. It only truly comes to us, however, when we have plumbed our own depths, faced our own questions – however frightening, and when, as Stanislaus Kennedy asserts, 'we have met and accepted the best and worst in ourselves'. That ancient book of Chinese wisdom, the I Ching, makes the same point. Once you have looked honestly into your own heart and your own motives, you will never again fear any heart that comes from outside yourself. If I make this process sound simple I apologise. The pitfalls are many. It is easy to pretend to yourself that you have performed this inner searching when all you have really done is make a few scratch marks on the impervious surface of your protective ego."

Johnnie was driving Sarah back home at Fina's request, having gently told the veil's newest recruit that her numerous other questions must wait for a while to be answered. "It is a lot to take in," Sarah admitted to Johnnie. "This secret society of good people existing independently of state governments and ideologies – how mind-boggling! My dad speaking on their behalf as if he had never died! Everything about Fina challenges my credulity. Humanity is so obtuse, fearful, and in denial. Can such a tiny international organisation, however enlightened, really turn the tanker round as it heads for the rocks?" Johnnie spotted a full moon in the night sky as he replied, "I've never met anyone with so pure an energy aura as Fina. It makes me trust in her confidence implicitly."

Nearby in a residential house Williamson was scribbling on a sheet of paper. He gulped down a fourth large whiskey. Then, tearing the pages he had been reading out of the book, stuffed them desperately into an envelope together with the scribble and brusquely addressed it to Sarah Atkinson.

HEAVEN AND EARTH

 It was an hour after high water at The London Apprentice, Donna sipping lemonade as she sketched, Mike engrossed in *The Observer*. "96 brothels exploiting immigrant women have now come to light in the Vice Squad's biggest ever UK operation," Mike read out. "The two men in custody, Christopher La Frayne and Richard Weller, are believed to be heads of an international syndicate."

Donna reflected on the names. One rang a vague bell. "Did I mention I received a letter from Australia?" she said. "It's from Anthony Orwell, the artist who had the exhibition at The Tate. He heard about me on the Internet and has given me an open invitation to visit him over there. It's very odd really. He mentioned how beautiful Australian butterflies are and suggested I might love to paint them." Donna gazed pensively up river. "What's odd about that?" asked Mike. "Well, when I was little we had a neighbour called Tony," she replied.

"He used to make butterflies. He even gave me one – Look! What's that?"

Mike shifted his gaze in the direction Donna's pencil pointed. A dark bulky object had drifted close to the wharf. "Go and investigate!" she ordered and as Mike obeyed Donna's quixotic fingers translated his efforts of retrieval onto paper. After five minutes he suddenly turned towards her and came sprinting back towards the pub terrace. "Phone the police!" he shouted. "It's a dead body!"

Fina had arrived with Johnnie at Sarah's shortly before 2pm. "I went to your home in Clapham once," Fina recalled. "Just after Don's death. You must have been at school, Sarah. Your mum had decided to incinerate all Don's possessions but I managed to persuade her to give me the notebooks." Sarah stopped pouring the drinks. "Incinerate them? But why?" she exclaimed. "The notebooks represented the past," replied Fina, "and your mum wanted to put a line under it. She needed to move on. That was her way of coping."

Sarah retreated into her own thoughts. "I'd like you to accompany Johnnie to California on

Friday," Fina continued at an appropriately judged moment. "He's going to have his psychic abilities thoroughly evaluated at The Institute of Noetic Science and I want him out of the way until the Weller prosecution is over, just in case Johnnie's inculcated. What do you say, Sarah? I'm sure we can persuade your college employer to give you leave of absence."

Sarah expressed reservations. "That case might not come to the high court for ages," she conjectured but when Johnnie confessed how much he would value her companionship Sarah was finally persuaded to cooperate with the plan. "I suppose it's my duty as a new recruit to your underground organisation, Fina," she said. "But how do I otherwise fit in? I mean do you intend me to have a distinctive role or what?"

"Right now your role is to keep running The Unreasonable Club," suggested Fina. "As the Buddhist said, 'Before enlightenment chop wood and carry water. After enlightenment chop wood and carry water.' The organisation's financial and moral support is a given. But first take a fortnight's holiday. You've more than earned it!"

Sarah smiled but still looked a bit disconcerted. "What's wrong?" asked Johnnie. Sarah pointed at an envelope on the table. "This came in the mail yesterday," she said. "Take a look."

Even before he withdrew the contents, three pages of *Heaven and Earth* plus a scrawled note, Johnnie felt through his sensitive finger tips the suicidal despair it contained, the inebriated self-disgust. *Dear Sarah*, he read, *apart from Martelli the most perceptive people I've ever come across are your father and Jeanette Winterson, in that order. Of course I had to kill Don [who wouldn't, such a remarkable talent?] but like most things I attempted in my life [including the seduction of your mother who I came to love with unquenchable passion and still do] I utterly failed. It was just as you witnessed it, a freak road accident, nothing more. Let this be my epitaph. 'Those who unflinchingly believe in heaven go to heaven when they die. Those who unflinchingly believe in oblivion go there instead.' When you read this, therefore, I shall be 'oblivious'. Trust the words of a dying man. There is only one person I hated more than Don and that is me. You have forced me finally to stop denying it to myself. Don was my proxy self. My surrogate. My nemesis. He succeeded at the "feeling" thing whereas I failed, - in fact I never even tried. JW writes, 'Nobody can feel too much though many work very hard at feeling too little'. [me] 'Our feelings can be so unbearable that we employ ingenious strategies, unconscious strategies, to keep those feelings away.' [me again] 'The psyche is much smarter than consciousness allows. We bury things so deep, we no longer remember there was anything to bury. Our neurotic states remember. But we don't.' [me and thrice me] Yours, Martin Williamson.*

Within the next 24 hours police reports confirmed Williamson's body had been in the river for three days and floated down from Hammersmith Bridge where a nocturnal stroller had witnessed a distant figure jumping. "At least he had a conscience, if not quite a soul," Mike told Donna who had only known Williamson as a celluloid image in her baptism photograph. Donna asked Johnnie to psycho-metrically sense the character of Anthony Orwell from the letter he'd sent her. Without reading it Johnnie pronounced, "The writer was once almost dead at sea. His injuries have been considerable. But now he is reborn and happy." And these uncanny words brought tears of nostalgia flowing from Donna's eyes.

When Fina saw Sarah alone the next day she confided how pernicious and unethical Williamson had been in his practice of psycho-therapy. "I know because I was his mentor for a while just after he completed his training," she said. He had encouraged emotional depen-dency in his clients rather than autonomous growth because he needed their uncritical esteem to fill the void in his own psyche. Entirely cerebral and analytical in his methodology, Williamson's own heart springs appeared to have dried up in adolescence. Love to him was about jealous possession and animal lust. Don had once told him words to the same effect, thereby consolidating Williamson's enmity for life."

"But Don's childhood had also been emotion-ally impoverished," Fina explained, "as the consequence of a bullying macho father and timid, acquiescent mother. Don's first loving relationship was with another boy, a fact he kept secret from your mum, Margaret, for ages. He was never confidant in his sexual orientation and that is basically why he split up with my daughter, Penny. They remained close friends. I counselled Don for months. And he eventually came to realise during therapy that his flings with other women were cries for help and affirmation. This is not to excuse him. He hurt your mum even though he loved her deeply and genuinely."

Sarah wanted to know if Penny had secretly remained Don's lover after she became married to Richard Weller. "Absolutely not, I'm positive about that," replied Fina. "That was what Weller chose to believe. Beneath the layered charm Weller turned out to be - well, a dangerously warped misogynist. He knocked Penny around terribly. When she finally plucked up the courage to leave with the children I was on secondment in The States. She went into a refuge and I asked Don to support her. She became very dependent on Don and when he so tragically died the shock tipped Penny over the edge and she took an overdose of valium. Weller went his own sweet way to the Far East and I brought up their children."

On the way home Sarah considered Fina's amazing qualities of resilience and optimism. She also reflected on how deeply this journey into her father's lost life had profited her. "Reality is totally different for the spectator and the participant," Fina had counselled. "When you wholeheartedly participate in reality, reality changes. Heaven and Earth are the same place experienced through different lenses of expectation."

The next morning Mike drove Donna at her request down the motorway network towards Guildford and a beauty spot on the ridge of the North Downs known as Newlands Corner. She had been there before and always enjoyed the challenge the Surrey hills imposed on her landscaping skills. Mike had some serious summer reading to keep him busy so he left Donna to her own artistic devices on a high rim of the valley while he retired with his books for a late breakfast at the café some 400 yards distant. A blissful warmth caressed the countryside. Above her head a few fleecy clouds dappled the vast canopy of sky and the verdant green pastures seemed to be riding up on a heat haze to greet them. She set up her easel and watercolours to paint but the sheer power of nature stayed her hand. And as she gazed outwards so the North Downs moved inexorably from beyond her to within. These rolling hills were her dwelling place and she became theirs.

When Mike eventually rejoined her bearing a gift of ice-cold lemonade she did not notice his presence. He looked at the blank sheet of paper and scoffed, "You've not done much! In fact nothing at all! Are you waiting for inspiration?"

These words were sufficient to awake Donna from the trance into which she had fallen. Her mouth and tongue rediscovered their function and she tried to speak. "It has happened before," Mike heard her say, "but never like this."

"Like what?" demanded Mike so earnestly that Donna literally fell down on the ground consumed with laughter at the ridiculousness of it all. "Donna? Have you hurt yourself?" asked Mike bending over her. 'Donna? Like what? Tell me!"

"My sense of who I am," she managed at last, "I mean as something solid, it just disappeared. The space between me and these hills and sky, earth and heaven, just dropped away and I dissolved into it, Mike. The world – where did it go?"

Mike propped her up then tried to lift her dead weight in his arms all the while coaxing, "Come along, Donna. You must have banged your head. We need to get you to a hospital."

That evening Joanne came round for a drink with Sarah and they ended up watching *Question Time* on television because Fina was scheduled to be a panellist. "No wild parties while I'm away in The States," Sarah lectured her sister, "and no eloping with swivel-eyed strangers." Donna who had fully recovered from her Samadhi encounter with the Absolute pulled a petulant face. "This programme's boring!" she complained. And for a while she proved right. Bombastic predominantly male egos jousting blunt-edged mediocre opinions about a range of geopolitical and social problems with the occasional isolated pause for wisdom. Then someone in the audience asked,

"To what extent have four waves of feminist agitation created radical permanent change in our male dominated culture?"

The answers went the same predictably complacent, preening way. "Excellent progress but there's still room for improvement, of course!" But then Lord Flitchson, a Tory grandee, spoke. Joanne giggled, knowing him from old as one of her more submissive tricks. "What some women call 'patriarchy' will always survive intact as the dominant ideology," he droned pompously, "simply because men are the physically stronger gender group and will never be persuaded to relinquish anything but the meagre crumbs of their power. And frankly why should they? To become a leader women need to display tougher and more masculine traits than men! A paradox, tragic though it may be, that can never be resolved."

After the snickering applause the chair turned to Professor Martelli who said with a wry smile, "One day a frog jumped into a bucket of milk and could not get out. The sides were far too steep and slippery and high. She tried everything, deep diving, leaping, propelling her feet off the base and nothing worked. Still it was exercise and good fun at that and so the frog refrained from giving up. 'There has to be a way!' she exhorted herself with a laugh and continued kicking and gyrating against the seemingly impossible odds. Eventually all this churning miraculously turned the milk into a solid hunk of butter and out the frog climbed."

Afterword

Although this is a work of fiction, I have tried to give credit within the text to all those authentic thinkers whose ideas have helped me in the construction of this novel. If I have missed anyone out I apologise for the oversight. I also need to acknowledge my appreciation of the writers referenced here with whom I substantively disagree. They too make an important contribution to the contemporary discourse.

Lightning Source UK Ltd.
Milton Keynes UK
UKOW04f2148161114

241668UK00004B/10/P